*new sounds for woodwind*

# new sounds

## BRUNO BARTOLOZZI

translated and edited by Reginald Smith Brindle

# *for woodwind*

*Second edition*

LONDON

*OXFORD UNIVERSITY PRESS*
NEW YORK · TORONTO
1982

*Oxford University Press, Walton Street, Oxford* OX2 6DP

OXFORD   LONDON   GLASGOW   NEW YORK
TORONTO   MELBOURNE   AUCKLAND   CAPE TOWN
NAIROBI   DAR ES SALAAM   TOKYO   KUALA LUMPUR
SINGAPORE   JAKARTA   HONG KONG   DELPHI
BOMBAY   CALCUTTA   MADRAS   KARACHI

© Oxford University Press 1967, 1982

ISBN 0 19 318611 X

*First edition published* 1967

*Second edition first published* 1982

The cover photograph is from an oscilloscope reading of part of the record supplied with this book.

British Library Cataloguing in Publication Data

Bartolozzi, Bruno
  New sounds for woodwind. – 2nd ed.
  1. Woodwind instruments
  I. Title   II. Brindle, Reginald Smith
  788'.05'0712    MT339    80-40519

ISBN 0-19-318611-X

Reset and printed in England by
Ebenezer Baylis and Son Limited
The Trinity Press, Worcester, and London

# contents

# acknowledgements

My greatest thanks are due to Sergio Penazzi, without whose help this book could never have been written. Professor Penazzi, who is first bassoon player at the Teatro alla Scala and teacher at the Milan Conservatoire, showed me how multiple sounds could be played on the bassoon as long ago as 1960, and since then has given me full collaboration in evolving new techniques. Later, Lawrence Singer confirmed that similar results are possible with oboe and also conducted experiments in methods of quarter-tone production. The validity of these techniques for all other woodwind instruments was then confirmed with the help of players in the Maggio Musicale Orchestra of Florence.

My most sincere thanks are therefore due to Sergio Penazzi and Lawrence Singer for their untiring assistance and collaboration, and for those players of the Maggio Musicale Orchestra who helped me so much, particularly the flautist Pierluigi Mencarelli and the clarinettist Detalmo Corneti. Finally, I would like to thank Reginald Smith Brindle for his precious contribution in preparing this book in an original version in English.

For the second edition, while expressing my profound thanks once again to the eminent instrumentalists Sergio Penazzi, Lawrence Singer, Pierluigi Mencarelli, and Detalmo Corneti, I wish also to express my gratitude to the clarinettist Giuseppe Garbarino for the most invaluable co-operation he gave me in carrying out further instrumental researches and in formulating the relevant technical details set out in this book. And I wish once more to acknowledge the decisive encouragement and assistance I have received from Reginald Smith Brindle from the earliest beginnings up to the present.

BRUNO BARTOLOZZI

*editor's note*

Bruno Bartolozzi died while this second edition was in proof. The numerous detailed changes since the original publication were, however, mostly made during his lifetime, and the final text is believed to conform with his intentions.

REGINALD SMITH BRINDLE

# *1 preliminary observations*

Wenn es Wirklichkeitssinn gibt, muss es auch Moglichkeitssinn geben. ROBERT MUSIL

The event which distinguishes the present musical age is the discovery of the means of producing music electronically. A new period has begun in which traditional instruments are no longer the uncontested protagonists of the musical scene. Orchestral instruments are now set against electronic devices, such as elaborators, computers, synthesizers, etc., capable of producing sounds which for structural reasons they themselves cannot. These devices, besides being able to produce the whole range of sounds that can be achieved by conventional instruments, are also able to produce a vast number of other sounds, in practice the whole range of frequencies that is theoretically possible. This development has been of enormous musical importance, and has had a profound effect on the life of the instruments themselves. Contrary to some prophecies of their gradual abandonment they are receiving instead a great impetus of technical development, largely stimulated by the example set by electronic devices. In fact we owe to electronic music the revelation of a world of sounds unknown to instrumental music, at the moment when traditional instruments were considered to have reached the limits of their technical possibilities. This revelation has helped greatly to develop a musical situation so much in ferment as it is today, in which the present progress of instruments seems perfectly natural. For this reason our own instrumental researches may be seen as a not unfruitful labour.

The field of research that has been opened up with *New Sounds for Woodwind* is vast, so much so that it was clearly not possible to explore it all in a single investigation. This second edition of the book therefore has the aim of providing more information about the technical possibilities that have already been discussed, and of illustrating others, so as to facilitate the completion of the research and hence the introduction into instrumental practice of the sounds resulting from the newly-acquired techniques. In trying to attain this goal we shall combine the experience gained from preparing four tutors[1] with the observations and comments which have been made to us by numerous instrumentalists and composers.

It first became clear that further developments in woodwind techniques can be achieved when it was found that certain new playing techniques led to effects of unexpected novelty. Since then a substantial vocabulary of new sounds has been formed which can enrich and amplify that which already exists.

Researches began with a discovery of fundamental importance, that woodwind instruments—contrary to general belief—can produce multiple sounds. Furthermore, these multiple sounds can be organized into polyphonic writing.[2] Such a possibility has so far been completely ignored both in orthodox instrumental usage and by those who have published treatises on the acoustical characteristics of wind instruments. This possibility of producing a rich vocabulary of multiple sounds means that up till now only a part (and perhaps not the most interesting part) of the real resources of the woodwind have been exploited.

Such a discovery reveals that the real capabilities of these instruments are twofold—both monophonic and multiphonic (and not, as has always been supposed, only monophonic)—and naturally technical developments will now turn towards a more complete exploitation of these resources.

---

[1] For flute by Pierluigi Mencarelli; for oboe by Lawrence Singer; for clarinet by Giuseppe Garbarino; for bassoon by Sergio Penazzi—Edizioni Suvini Zerboni, Milan.

[2] 'Polyphony', as here used, is meant not so much in the academic sense of strict contrapuntal usage, but in a wider sense signifying 'many-voiced' sounds organized in such a way as to be of musical significance.

Elsewhere in this book the hybrid term 'multiphonic' has had to be coined in order to describe the general concept of multiple sounds produced by woodwind (as opposed to their normal production of single sounds). The author always refers to 'polyphonic' possibilities in the original Italian, but it has been felt best to avoid this usage (with its inference of organized voice writing), even if an ungainly-looking substitute has had to be resorted to. (Ed.)

As in this treatise there is no proposal to modify the existing structure of woodwind instruments—a structure 'which science itself holds to be so excellent as to discourage any modifications'[1]—it would be legitimate to ask why traditional techniques have not included all those resources which instruments really have to offer. How is it that, until today, possibilities which have always existed, have been so long ignored? How is it that instrumental techniques have become fixed in a pattern which does not allow any results except those actually in conventional use? The complex issues behind these questions are such that straightforward, irrefutable answers cannot be given. However, suppositions can be made which must be fairly near the truth of the matter.

On examining the historical development of woodwind instruments, there appear to be two main reasons which have determined traditional techniques. One is that the structural evolution of instruments has been derived by exclusively empirical methods, the other reason has been the musical requirements of past epochs. In fact, as both instrument-makers and performers have not followed (or have not been able to follow) scientific directives indicating the ends to pursue, their efforts have been concentrated on a single objective—the emission of single sounds of maximum timbric homogeneity throughout the range of instruments.[2] The objective has therefore been not one of exploiting the characteristic possibilities of each instrument but of satisfying the musical requirements of each successive epoch. If this empirical procedure has produced excellent results from the structural point of view, it is evident that the same cannot be said as regards the development of technique, which has become rigidly standardized in one method aimed at the most efficient achievement of the original objective—single sounds of homogeneous timbre.

However, in the development of woodwind instruments one

---

[1] Ottavio Tiby, *Acustica Musicale* (Palermo, 1933), p. 177.
[2] We refer to 'single' sounds here and later on knowing full well that instruments do not produce single sounds but a principal tone and also additional partial tones which give the sound its particular timbre. However, we are accustomed to hear these as single sounds, and we will continue to refer to them as such in order to differentiate them from multiple sounds which are indubitably heard as combinations of different notes. (Ed.)

scientific approach of no small importance has been used, that of taking advantage of the acoustic principle on which the 'mixed' system of sound production is based. This 'mixed' system comprises a range of *fundamental* tones in the lower register of instruments and their various *harmonics* from which higher notes are derived. The upper registers of woodwind instruments are completed by using partial tones from the harmonic series whose wavelengths are integral fractions of those of the various fundamentals ($\frac{1}{2}$, $\frac{1}{3}$, $\frac{1}{4}$, $\frac{1}{5}$, and $\frac{1}{6}$).[1] These partial tones are harmonics at the octave, twelfth, double octave, seventeenth, and nineteenth respectively, and are used in this order to form the upper registers—an order which is *pre-established and never altered*. Such a procedure, though excellent as regards satisfying the traditional demand for single sounds of homogeneous timbre, is indeed something of an obstacle when we wish to obtain those other effects which these instruments can really produce.

In fact, the use of a single pre-established order of harmonics in the 'mixed' system of sound production has led to the establishment of a single system of fingerings caused by the selection—from a large number of alternative fingerings—of only those which are most suitable to ensure good intonation and the maximum of timbric unity throughout the range of each instrument. Admittedly, a limited number of alternative fingerings have been established with a view to facilitating certain passages or (in the upper register) the emission of difficult notes, but the general intention has been one of standardization and the elimination of alternatives. Similarly, the embouchure and blowing techniques have also been standardized so as to ensure timbric uniformity, resulting in an unvaried, standard type of performing technique.

These are the causes which have made traditional techniques become a closed system, a system which deliberately excludes any pos-

---

[1] These are the partial tones used in a cylindrical tube open at both ends (the flute) or a tapered cone effectively closed at one end (the oboe and bassoon). With the clarinet, however, which is a cylindrical tube effectively closed at one end, only odd-numbered partials are available (i.e. $\frac{1}{3}$, $\frac{1}{5}$, $\frac{1}{7}$, and $\frac{1}{9}$). These represent harmonics at the twelfth, seventeenth, twenty-first, and twenty-third respectively, notes which bear relationships of one octave and a fifth, and two octaves and a third, seventh, and ninth with the fundamental. (Ed.)

sibility which does not contribute to its own objectives, and thereby eliminates from the outset so many other latent possibilities which we are only now discovering. This situation has been quite satisfactory as long as musical requirements were limited to the purity and 'beauty' of sound obtained through uniformity of timbre. But such ideals have become more and more inadequate to the needs of contemporary music. For while it is legitimate to disregard that maltreatment of instruments which occurs in some kinds of 'artistic' manifestations, it is nevertheless true that contemporary music requires means of expression which can no longer be exclusively provided by 'beauty' of sound or 'tunefulness'. In fact, as there are no longer 'false' notes now that the electronic sound spectograph has allowed the frequency of any sound to be determined, so there are no longer sounds which are 'ugly', 'unpleasant', 'hard', etc. Rather are there only sound phenomena which are useful in proportion to how much they lend themselves to organized musical usage.

It is precisely in this direction that those more adventurous instrumentalists have directed their efforts in their search for new sounds designed to satisfy the needs of contemporary composers.

As became apparent from the beginning of our investigations, we can now confirm that the most fruitful field for research lies in the following instrumental possibilities: (a) the suitability of woodwind for the creation of single sounds with marked difference of timbre; (b) the ability of these instruments to play music which contains smaller intervals than those contained in the tempered chromatic scale; (c) the suitability of each instrument for creating polyphony, that is, not only the emission of very varied combinations of chords, but the execution of a true and proper instrumental polyphony.

Other possibilities will be discussed later, but from the above alone it is evident that there exists a well-founded escape route from the restrictions of the fixed traditional techniques. This route may be followed by examining all the means of sound production *de novo*, without setting any limits to our objectives, and only aiming at exploiting whatever sound phenomena are discovered, in a musicianly manner. The objective of this book is therefore one of illustrating the technical development of the real resources of woodwind, as well as providing a large number of musical illustrations of all the technical possibilities discussed, to allow the immediate use of the resulting new sounds. I must confirm that the results of investigations have been arrived at only by practical experiment and not through scientific research. (This is inevitable, for it would seem that at the moment scientific research into woodwind sound-phenomena lags very much behind the practice which this treatise proposes. To have attempted scientific researches would have slowed down these investigations very drastically, though it is to be hoped that in time science will furnish explanations for many perplexing phenomena.) Given the empirical nature of the researches, it is therefore proposed to use only conventional musical and instrumental terminology in this book. Due to the lack of scientific principles and because of the complexity and novelty of the subject-matter, it would be absurd to pretend to establish irrefutable theories. On the contrary, where theories are advanced, their purpose is rather that of permitting an immediate practical application of general principles.

In order that the reader may be introduced to the more complex subject of multiple sounds by easy steps which begin with the study of single sounds, the treatment of monophonic possibilities has at first been separated from multiphonic phenomena. We will therefore keep to the following scheme: the second chapter will deal with monophonic possibilities, the third with multiple sounds and polyphony and the fourth will demonstrate the whole of these possibilities, monophonic and multiphonic, brought together in one unified technique.

Rather than deal with woodwind instruments of every kind, it has been thought sufficient to deal only with the main representatives of each group—flute, oboe, clarinet, and bassoon. The technical possibilities of all the others can be logically deduced from following that of the four main types.

Before examining *de novo* the monophonic possibilities of woodwind instruments it is necessary to establish some rules of a general nature. It is necessary to specify (1) what is the real nature and quantity of fingerings available so as to establish a method of investigation, (2) how the monophonic and multiphonic possibilities are distributed in the compass of instruments, (3) how to adapt the embouchure and method of blowing to the needs of the new techniques.

*Fingerings available*

Theoretically, the number of possible fingerings available is enormous, for it is the result of all the possible combinations of finger and thumb holes multiplied by all the possible combinations of chromatic keys. For example:

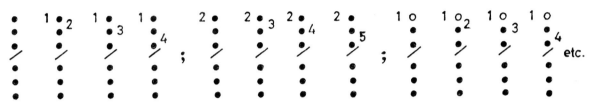

(N.B.—The fingering systems used in this treatise are the Boehm Systems for the flute and clarinet, the Conservatory System for the oboe and the Heckel System for the bassoon. These are indicated on the diagrams of instruments included as a foldout at the end of the book.)

In theory this provides many millions of possible fingerings, but in practice many of them give an identical sound result. Nevertheless, the number of fingerings is so great as to discourage at the outset any method which contemplates the investigation of every available fingering one by one. The problem should rather be limited to devising the best way of selecting fingerings for any specific purpose, in which case the most practical procedure would be as follows:

*a.* decide on a limited technical objective which our knowledge of the monophonic and multiphonic possibilities of any instrument may suggest;

*b.* devise the method of selection of suitable fingerings;

*c.* adapt the embouchure and mode of blowing as necessary;

*d.* classify the sound material obtained.

*Distribution of monophonic and multiphonic characteristics throughout the compass of instruments*

It must be first established at which point in the compass of instruments the same sound can be emitted with tone-colours of distinctly different quality. In other words, the lowest note from which it is possible to generate the same fundamental soundwave with different percentages of its various upper partials. This begins at the point of the compass in which the same sound can be played with different fingerings[1] and is at the low G♯ for the flute, low D♯ on the oboe, low A (as written) on the clarinet and low C on the bassoon. Below these notes, it is impossible to play sounds with more than one fingering, but higher up, alternative fingerings are available, often in very abundant quantity.

It is from this same point that instruments are able to emit combinations of chords containing from two to six sounds, that is, they can generate simultaneously a number of frequencies of vibration the lowest of which is not necessarily a simple fraction of all the others.[2] Particularly worthy of note is the clarinet, which, in contrast to the other instruments, can form chordal combinations even from the lowest fundamental.

We can therefore establish—even if only by practical experiment—that the dual capacity (monophonic/multiphonic) of woodwind instruments begins at the notes specified above, continuing uninterruptedly throughout the rest of the compass, except for the clarinet as mentioned. Virtually the whole range of instruments is available, except for the lowest fundamentals indicated. This does not exclude the possibility that all instruments (particularly the oboe and bassoon) may have multiphonic resources from the lowest fundamentals, but, as it is preferable to consider only what has been achieved in practice, this eventuality must for the moment be shelved.

[1] These various fingerings naturally do not include those which merely use alternative *keys* which can be used by fingers of either hand to close the same hole (as the clarinet).
[2] If the lowest sound were a simple fraction of the frequencies of higher notes, we would have a sound combination comprising a fundamental and certain of its upper partials. This, in fact, is quite possible, as certain sounds can be created which include only major or minor chords. But more frequently the situation is much more complex and the lowest sound seems to bear little or no frequency relationship to the others.

LIST OF SIGNS USED TO INDICATE EMBOUCHURES,
LIP PRESSURES, AIR PRESSURES, ETC.

## Lip pressures

○  =  relaxed lip pressure
◕  =  slightly relaxed lip pressure
●  =  very relaxed lip pressure[1]
□  =  increased lip pressure
◪  =  slightly increased lip pressure
■  =  much increased lip pressure

## Air pressures

N.Pr.  =  normal air pressure
M.Pr.  =  much pressure
P.Pr.  =  little pressure
A.Pr.  =  augment air pressure
D.Pr.  =  diminish air pressure

In general, where dynamic signs correspond to the blowing pressure required, eg.

there is no need to add specific indications for increased (or decreased) air pressure, as these are already implicit in the dynamic symbols

---

[1] In the case of the clarinet the inside of the lower lip should rest on the reed instead of on the teeth as in the normal lip position.

used. But special use of lip and air pressures may be required (and must be indicated) where the dynamics of the music do not imply any change, as, for example:

*Embouchures* (position of the lips on the reed)
    For reed instruments, these are shown as follows:

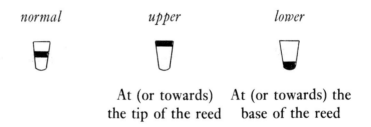

The sign ⤵ indicates that the instrument should be brought nearer the body so that the lower lip can press on the reed while the upper lip maintains a light pressure. The sign ⤴ indicates that the instrument should be brought upwards so that the upper lip can press on the reed while the lower lip maintains a light pressure. This way of increasing lip pressure is particularly useful with the clarinet. In the case of the flute the following signs indicate the various apertures of the lips and the position of the sound hole of the instrument:

○ Very wide—as playing in the low register

◓ Wide—as used in the middle register

● Not so wide—as used in the upper register

■ Very small aperture—as used in the upper register

◪ Reduced aperture—as used in the middle register

□ Not so reduced aperture—as used in the low register

*Sound-hole position*

○ Moving the hole outwards from the lips

○ Moving the hole towards the lips

These signs are virtually the same as those used for lip pressures with the reed instruments, in order to avoid the confusion of a large number of different signs. For a similar reason, when there is a normally obvious relationship between two factors—e.g. increased lip pressure and increased air pressure—one sign only will be used.
This is equally valid for both the flute and reed instruments. In other cases, where lip and air pressure are in contrast to the normal usage (e.g. □ and M.Pr.), both signs have to be used.

In cases where normal playing conditions are obvious (or where adjustments are so minimal as to be readily foreseen by the player) no signs are used.

The symbol 'N.' is used to indicate a return to normal playing methods when otherwise it would not be obvious, and cancels out any previous special usage.

# 2 monophonic possibilities

Monophonic possibilities will now be investigated, establishing as a first objective the emission of sounds with the *maximum differentiation of timbre*.

## PRINCIPAL SOUNDS AND SECONDARY SOUNDS

It has already been stated that woodwind instruments are the only ones which use a 'mixed' system of sound production (i.e. fundamental tones for the lower register and various natural harmonics of these for the upper registers). This means, amongst other things, that while the fundamental tones are based by construction on the tempered chromatic scale, the harmonics, having the intonation of upper partials, will have a slightly different tuning—that of the natural scale. But it is not on these discrepancies of intonation that we must focus our attention, but on the impossibility, with this traditional 'mixed' system of sound production, of obtaining any sounds other than the fundamentals determined by the construction of the instrument, and their related harmonics.

The ability to produce sounds of different kinds has been regarded as the prerogative of string instruments which, as well as being able to produce natural harmonics on the open strings, can produce other harmonics by pressing the string against the fingerboard at one point and lightly touching it at another.

It should further be noted that in string instruments, beginning with the harmonic at the fifth position on the lowest string, each harmonic can be obtained in different ways, according to whether it is natural or artificial, according to whether it is considered, for example, as the second harmonic of one fundamental or the third of another, whether it is obtained from one string or another, etc.

But from the moment we indicated (in Chapter 1) that woodwind can generate the same fundamental with different percentages of harmonics,[1] it will have been clear that—by different means, but through the same cause—they can produce:

FUNDAMENTALS DETERMINED BY THE CONSTRUCTION OF THE INSTRUMENT and their related harmonics, and FUNDAMENTALS OBTAINED BY DIFFERENT FINGERINGS and their related harmonics.

From this it follows that we have the possibility of producing the same note with distinctly different timbres and therefore of making use of the various harmonics derived from these sound generators in the ways we shall see later.

This means that the old belief that the woodwind are a more limited instrumental medium compared with the strings is erroneous. Indeed, the real situation is reversed. In fact, if on a qualitative plane their possibilities are identical, on a quantitative plane the woodwind now reveal far more numerous possibilities. In confirmation of this statement, it is enough to mention that ninety-eight different fingerings have been found on the oboe for B above middle C, with a consequent large variety of tone colours.

When this example is extended to all the sounds throughout the compass of an instrument (though not all sounds have such a large number of possible fingerings, often indeed much less) we have a striking demonstration of the vast number of fingerings each instrument has available for the production of single sounds and for creating fundamental sounds.

---

[1] 'Different percentages of harmonics' implies a difference in the *volume* of the various harmonics—hence the different qualities of timbre of the various fundamentals. However, in many cases the normal harmonics are *suppressed* (sometimes completely) and less usual harmonics *enhanced* considerably. This produces not only an unusual tone colour but (as will be seen) combinations of harmonics which seem to bear little or no direct relationship with the fundamental. (Ed.)

But it must be noted that, because of their large number, not all sounds have such diverse percentages of harmonics that the human ear can differentiate each sound with ease. Indeed, many are hard to classify because of the very slight differences of intonation which occur. Yet it is certain that whatever the number of sounds available for producing sounds of different timbres or for the uses to be discussed in the chapter on multiphonic possibilities, that number will be far greater than the more meagre possibilities of the strings.

Having defined what are, for the moment, the real monophonic possibilities of the woodwind, the practical realization of some of these can now be discussed. Having shown that through the use of special fingerings it is possible to obtain the same sound with different timbres and that these sounds are to be considered fundamentals, we shall now give some examples of the same sounds produced by different fingerings, and of the harmonics which can be derived from each of them. For the reasons explained above, examples are chosen from those which are most significant in that each fingering given produces a very different result. These harmonics are obtained by slight modifications of embouchure, lip, and air pressure which will be more fully described later. For the moment it is sufficient to say that in general the lower harmonics can be played on reed instruments by slightly increased lip and air pressure and the use of a little more reed than usual. Higher sounds will need more and more lip and air pressure. For the flute, the lip aperture must be reduced and air velocity increased more and more to move from lower harmonics to higher ones, as is the normal playing practice.

Ex. 1.  *Harmonics obtained by different fingerings of the same note*

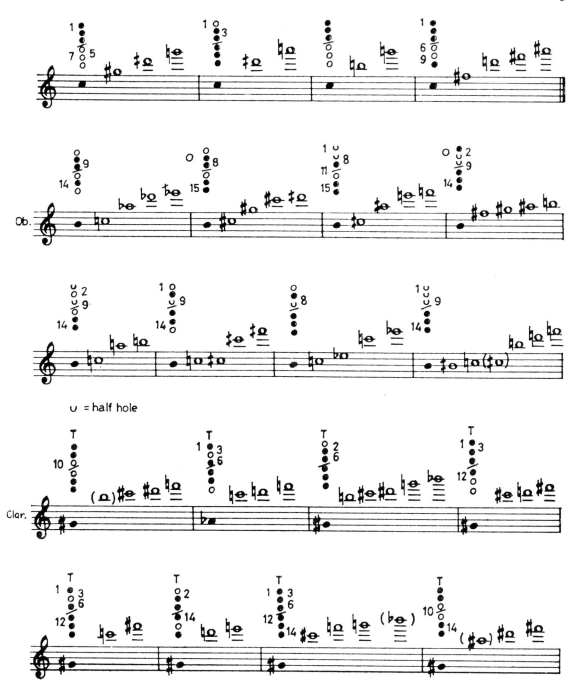

∪ = half hole

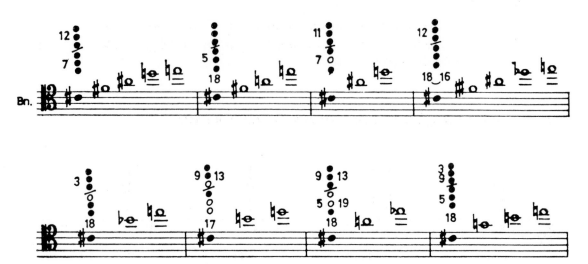

From these examples, though limited of necessity to different fingerings for a single note, it can be seen how the sequence of the harmonic series derived from the same fundamental can vary, with different percentages of its component harmonics. Thus it is evident that the possibility of obtaining different groups of harmonics from the same apparent fundamental leads to a full exploitation of many combinations of artificial harmonics. Just what this acquisition means will be explained in detail in the next chapter. For the moment, however, it is premature to digress into discussion of multiphonic effects and it is best to return to the classification of monophonic possibilities (using the sounds indicated in Ex. 1) and other connected issues.

CLASSIFICATION OF SINGLE SOUNDS ACCORDING TO TIMBRE

*a. Different timbres of the same note*
Though it is possible to produce a variety of tone colours for each note, in many cases the almost excessive number of different tone colours prevents an adequate descriptive definition of each timbre. Some of these have only very slight differences, subtle shadings which can certainly be used for greater colouristic effect, but here it is necessary to indicate only those timbres which have the most definite

characteristics and can be given an accurate descriptive term, thus leaving the performer to use other sounds of a slightly different colour as he wishes.

Ex. 2. *Classification of the most characteristic timbres of one note*

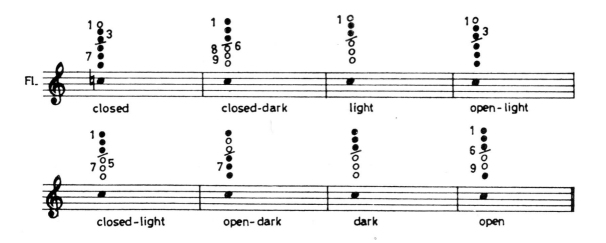

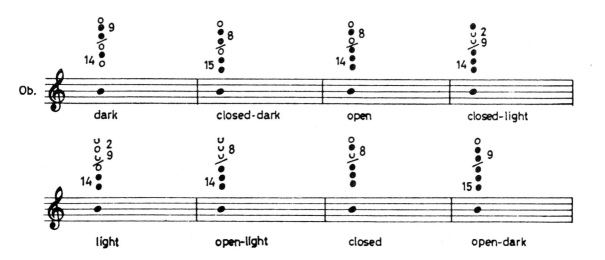

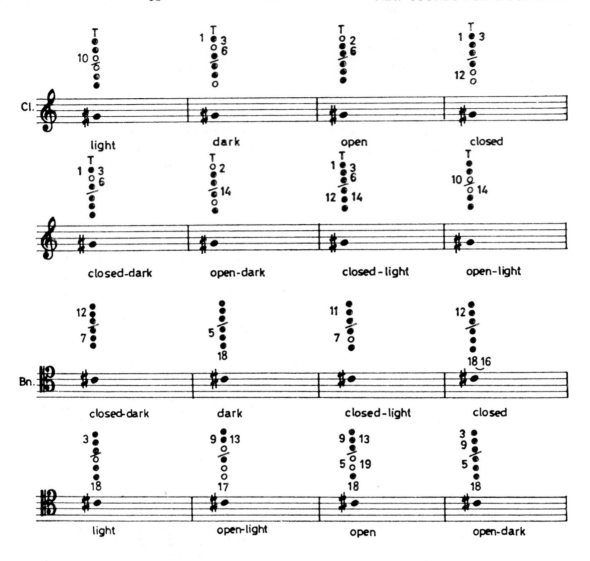

As can be seen, such a rich gamut of colouristic effects, obtained simply by using different fingerings, offers notable possibilities of using various timbres either on one note or on successions of notes of different pitch.

## b. *Timbric transformations of a sound*

We will now deal with the various effects obtained by transforming the timbre of a sound during its emission using various performing techniques.

### 1. *Changing the timbre of a sound*

This is achieved by using fingerings suitable for various tone colours during the emission of a sound held on one breath. Thus the sound, though uninterrupted, varies in colour at will.

Ex. 3.

∪ = half hole

### 2. The 'smorzato' sound

This is obtained by squeezing the reed with light movements of the lips caused in turn by corresponding movements of the jaw. The 'smorzato' is really a kind of vibrato, but instead of fluctuations of pitch (as in vibrato) the 'smorzato' consists of fluctuations in volume produced by the jaw and not by the diaphragm. Naturally the rhythmic pulse of the fluctuations can be timed by control of the jaw movements.

With the flute the 'smorzato' can be obtained by short staccati produced exclusively by the control of the diaphragm without the help of the tongue and throat as is necessary for normal staccato.

The 'smorzato' can be used throughout the entire compass of instruments, though it is of best effect in the middle and upper-middle registers. It is best used in a dynamic range which does not exceed mezzo forte, otherwise the sound becomes interrupted by the reed closing due to excessive air pressure. In the case of the flute the sound may be interrupted by excessive velocity of the air coupled with the movement of the player's lips.

*N.B.* The 'smorzato' sound is indicated by the white note.

Ex. 4.

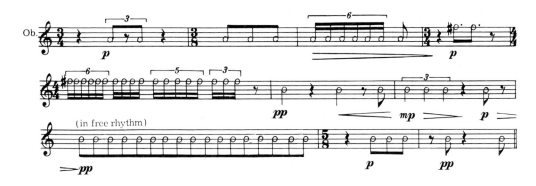

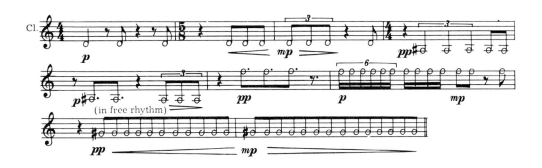

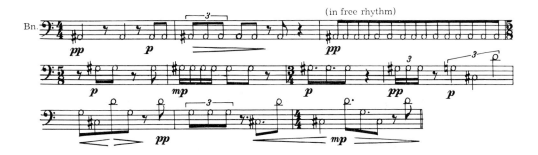

### 3. *The 'smorzato' coupled with various timbres*
This is obtained by combining the 'smorzato' effect with various fingerings which produce different tone colours.

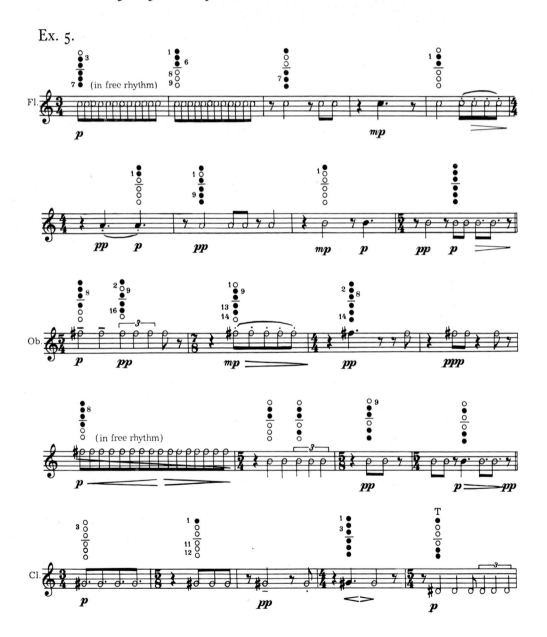

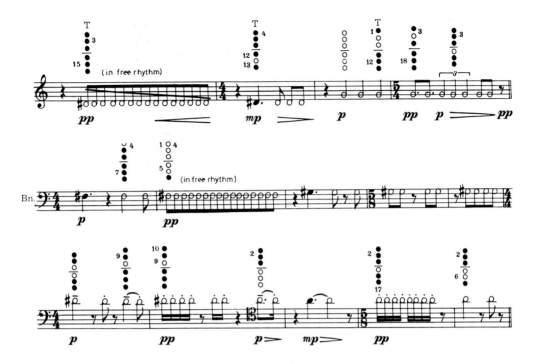

From these ways of transforming the timbre of sounds during their emission, effects can be obtained which are as suggestive as they are striking. Their fascination comes from the great variety of colouring derived from the changing colour spectrum of the sounds, the suffused sweetness of emission characterized by the 'smorzato', and finally the refined sculpturing of sounds which results from the combination of the two possibilities.

### c. Effects produced by lip control

From what has been revealed so far it is evident than an expert control of the embouchure and method of blowing is increasingly important. It is therefore necessary to regulate and control these aspects of execution in order to obtain the specific technical results so far mentioned and others which are to follow. Among these we must first consider the control of intonation with special reference to the use of vibrato and lip oscillations.

1. *Vibrato*

Control of vibrato is obtained by graduating the movement of the lips
while blowing from the diaphragm, such movements ranging in intensity from the minimum of non-vibrato to the maximum of vibratissimo. With the flute, vibrato can be produced by the lips or (as is
more commonly the case) by 'throat vibrato' in which movements
of the throat cause fluctuations in air pressure. However, throat vibrato is more suitable for a vibrato which ranges from medium intensity
to vibratissimo, while lip vibrato is suitable for a slower and more
gentle vibrato, producing slight changes in intonation (which throat
vibrato may not cause).

The symbols used to indicate various vibrati are as follows:

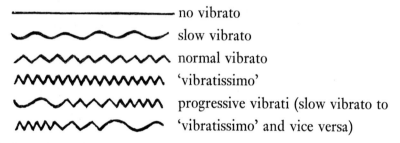

It is recommended that symbols for vibrati be placed below the
stave.

2. *Oscillations and half-oscillations*

Lip oscillations (by increasing and relaxing lip pressure) produce
fluctuations in intonation above and below the mean true pitch and
may be illustrated as follows:

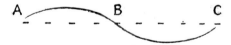

Here the dotted line indicates the mean pitch, segment AB indicates
a half-oscillation above this mean and segment BC below.

Such a lip movement, executed uniformly, produces half-oscillations of between a quarter and half a tone—above and below the mean
pitch—which can be used throughout the compass of instruments and
at any volume.

Alterations of a quarter-tone are indicated as follows:

♯ =quarter-tone sharp

♯♯ =three quarter-tones sharp

♭ =quarter-tone flat

♭ =three quarter-tones flat

Half-oscillation below:

Half-oscillation above:

Oscillation beginning below:

Oscillation beginning above:

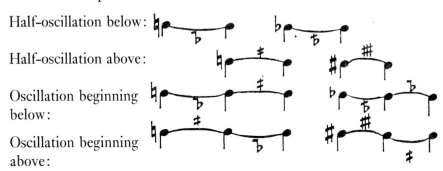

These accidental signs are best placed to the right of the note or notes concerned. It is advisable not to use more than four half-oscillations per beat at a normal tempo.

To clarify further the use that can be made of the effects produced by lip control, we give some practical examples of vibratos and oscillations.

Ex. 6.

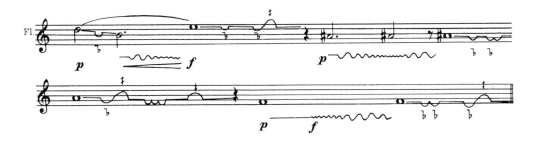

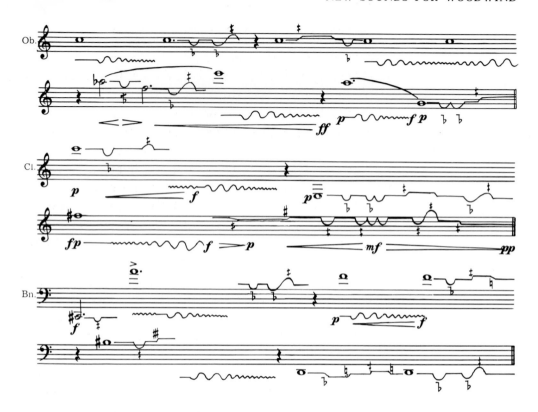

### QUARTER-TONES AND SMALLER INTERVALS

The above exposition of monophonic possibilities does not pretend to
be exhaustive. It has only highlighted those aspects of instrumental
usage which seem to offer the greatest field for development. So far,
however, only developments which lie within the confines of the
tempered chromatic scale of semitones have been considered. It will
be interesting to go on now to consider those possibilities woodwind
instruments offer in producing organized successions of sounds which
are closer together than the semitone.

Many years ago Schoenberg wrote: 'The efforts made here and
there to write music using one-third and quarter-tones are destined to
failure as long as the instruments capable of playing such music are so
few.'[1] Ever since Schoenberg wrote this, his statement has remained

[1] A. Schoenberg, *Harmonielehre* (Vienna, 1911).

substantially true, but as it is certain that the entire woodwind group are now available for music using such micro-intervals the position is surely changed. They seem to hold the key to a situation which has hung in the balance ever since Busoni wrote: 'The third of a tone has been knocking at our door for some time and we refuse to listen.'[1] Busoni himself, in his enthusiasm for the invention of Dr. Thaddeus Cahill,[2] believed that it was the destiny of electronic music to become a medium for music using one-third tones, but today it is clear that the problems which can be resolved electronically go far beyond the mere creation of such micro-intervals. But it is equally clear that these problems must not be confused with those of instrumental music. For the problems of instrumental music can only be solved through the medium of the instruments themselves.

Seeing that woodwind can emit sounds which are less than a semi-tone apart, these developments must be examined, and it is evident from the outset that their possibilities are considerable, since wood-wind can play intervals as small as one-eighth of a tone and one-sixth of a tone as well as the third- and quarter-tones already mentioned.

For the moment investigations must be concentrated on that in-terval which promises to be most useful (the quarter-tone), leaving aside the one-third of a tone, which is perhaps more interesting for the novel possibilities it offers, especially through the division of tones into three parts and the octave into eighteen equal parts. However, the quarter-tone promises for the moment to be more useful, because through introducing it the octave can be so conveniently divided into twenty-four equal parts, which can then be further subdivided so as to become forty-eight one-eighth tones if necessary.

Through this kind of subdivision, without throwing away the con-venience of equal temperament, a system can be formed which in some respects promises to be twice as rich as the present one.

Chromatic successions of quarter-tones can be obtained throughout the whole compass of instruments. They are not obtained through the

---

[1] *A New Aesthetic of Music* (Trieste, 1907).
[2] 'Dr. Thaddeus Cahill's Dinamophone, an extraordinary electrical invention for producing scientifically perfect music', by Ray Stannard Baker (*McClure's Maga-zine*, July 1906).

approximate method of lip adjustment, but through a well-defined
order of fingerings. Just as the chromatic scale of twelve semitones is
completed throughout the entire compass of instruments by the use
of fundamentals determined by the construction of the instrument
and their connected harmonics, similarly the octave can be subdivided
into twenty-four quarter-tones using fundamentals determined by
special fingerings and their related harmonics.

The quarter-tones thus obtained will have the same functions and
properties that have already been described for normal semitones.

As an explanation, we give the following examples:

Ex. 7. *Scales of quarter-tones throughout the main compass of instruments*

*Note*: There seem to be no fingerings suitable for the three notes F♯♯, G♯♯ and
A♯♯ in the low register. This is due to the coupling of various hole covers, normally
employed to provide alternative fingerings, which prevents us from using all possible fingering combinations. These could only be used if some means were provided
of uncoupling the various hole covers and finger plates without structurally modifying the instrument itself.

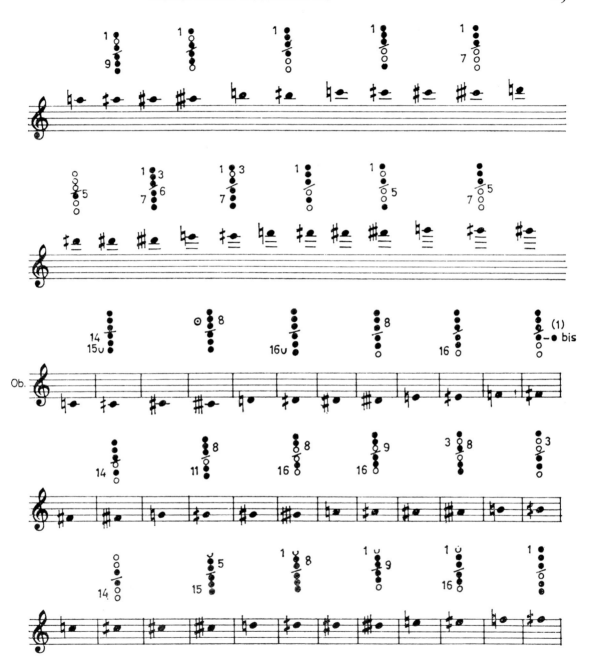

(1) indicates the small hole connected with the third hole in the centre.

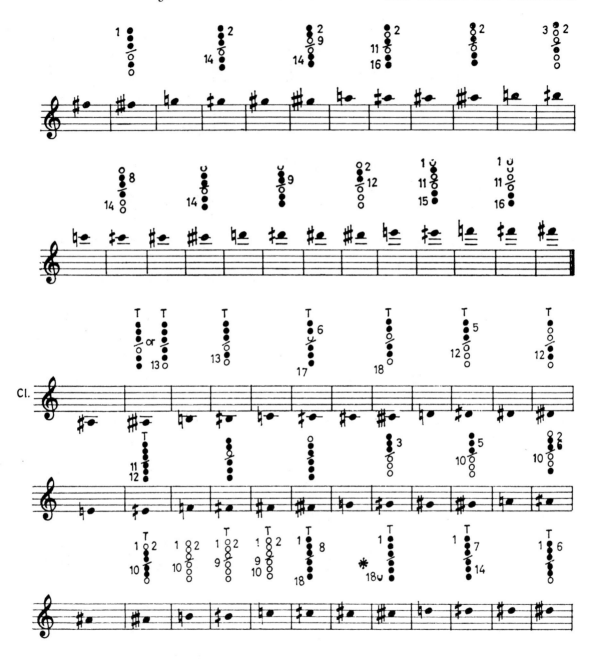

* quarter-open

Ex. 8. *Harmonics obtained by different fingerings of the same note*

Fl.

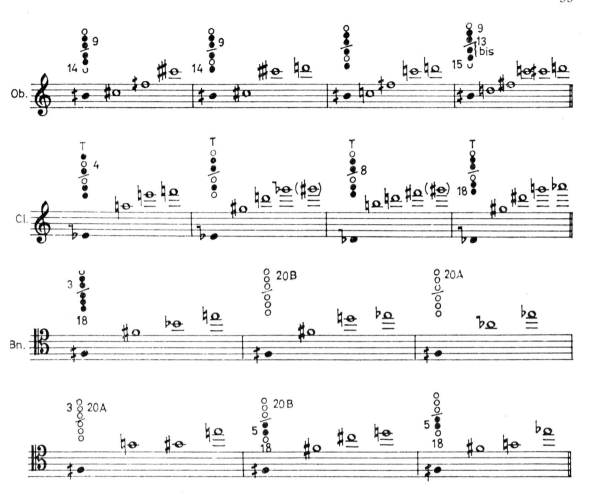

Ex. 9. *The same sound with different timbres*

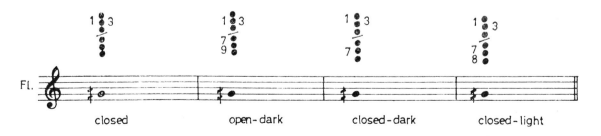

| closed | open-dark | closed-dark | closed-light |

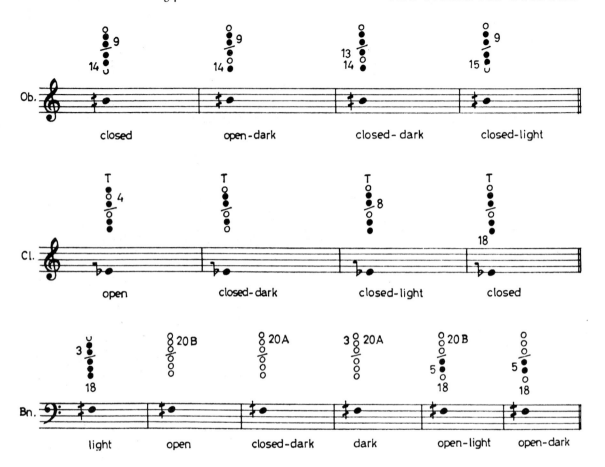

Since it is understood that all that has been said so far regarding the monophonic possibilities of semitones is equally valid for quarter-tones, we shall now proceed to examine other monophonic effects.

SPECIAL MONOPHONIC EFFECTS

*Portamento, upwards and downwards*

These are special portamenti between a sound and its next harmonic which are obtained by moving from the normal lip position to the next one, either above or below, and using appropriate fingerings.

Ex. 10.

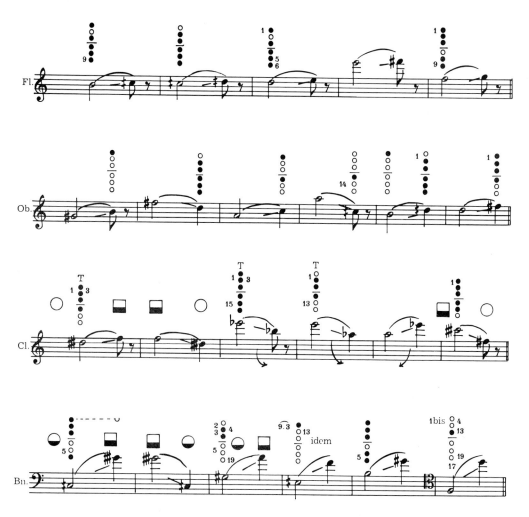

*Acciaccatura-portamento, upwards and downwards* (with the lips)

This is performed by moving rapidly from the normal lip position to the one either above or below at the moment of beginning the subsequent portamento. With the clarinet the acciaccatura is performed by rapidly releasing or squeezing the mouthpiece at the moment of beginning the subsequent portamento. In the case of the flute this effect is obtained because of the very nature of the instrument simply by increasing the wind pressure at the moment of beginning the small portamento. In every case this effect can be obtained only by using a special type of fingering, of which we give examples.

Ex. 11.

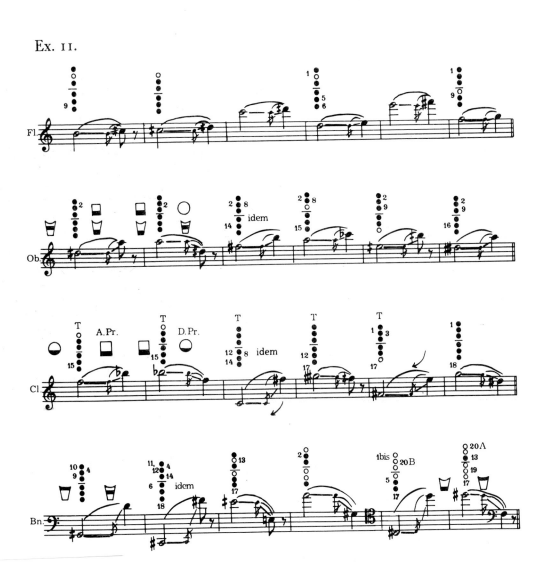

### *Acciaccatura-portamento, upwards and downwards* (by fingerings)

This is performed by adopting a second fingering, suitable for producing the initial note, at the moment of beginning the subsequent portamento. This effect, which is similar to the proceeding one but more refined, is thus obtained by a special use of fingerings and not of the lips.

Ex. 12.

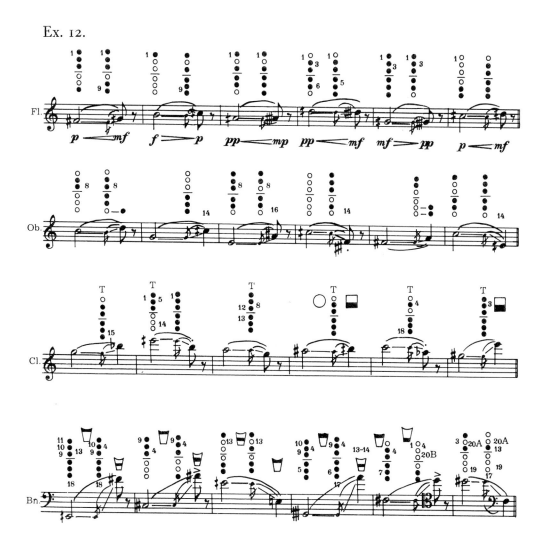

*The pedal key*

This is a method of giving tonal colouration to a phrase in cases where fingerings allow the use, as in a trill, of holes and keys which are not employed in the performance of the phrase itself. What is obtained in this way is not a true trill between one sound and another, but a continuous 'trilling' of sounds having the function of a pedal, which adds a special tone colour to the whole phrase.

Ex. 13.

*Glissando*

Since each instrument requires a different technique, we shall illustrate this effect separately.

FLUTE: glissando is obtained by co-ordinating the changes in the fingering indicated with the rotating movement imparted to the instrument from ◯ to ◯ , and with the increase in air pressure from P.Pr. to M.Pr. This type of upwards glissando can be performed only slowly and with a crescendo. The effect obtained is very interesting and extremely expressive.

Ex. 14.

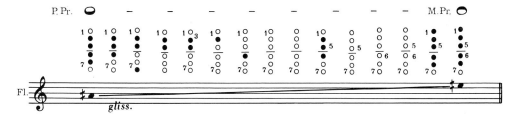

OBOE: glissando is obtained by sliding the fingers over the holes while moving from the first fingering to the second. In practice this is achieved by joining the two fingerings (initial and final) producing a progressive slide of the fingers which ensures the continuous movement necessary to maintain a uniform glissando either upwards or downwards. Naturally air pressure and lip pressure will be modified as necessary.

Ex. 15.

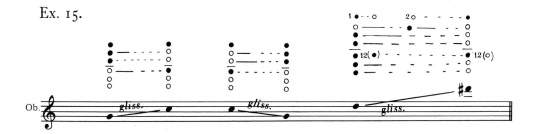

CLARINET: for this instrument the directions, because of their number, have been marked directly on the examples.

Ex. 16.

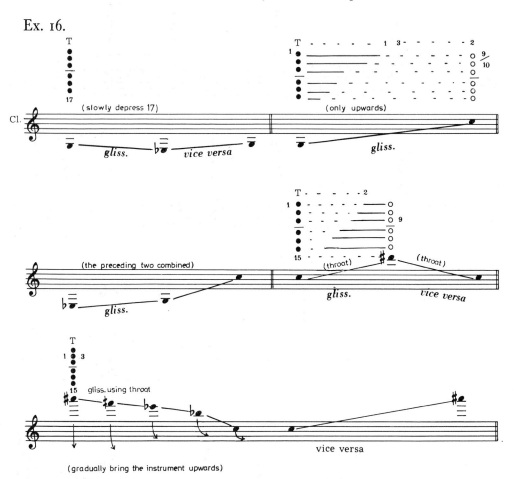

(gradually bring the instrument upwards)

BASSOON: in contrast to the portamenti already described, glissandi between single sounds are not possible on this instrument. However, as we shall see, they are possible between sound amalgams.

To conclude this chapter dealing with monophonic possibilities, we present some examples of quarter-tone melodies, which give an idea of the tonal coloration which is created spontaneously from the inherent natural differences in timbre between normal semitones and quarter-tones.

Ex. 17. *Succession of notes with different tone colours*

N.B. Where no fingerings are given, these are normal.

# 3 multiphonic possibilities

GENERAL CONSIDERATIONS

From what has already been said, it is evidently possible, without altering the structure of woodwind instruments in any way, to use various means of sound production, each depending on certain technical conditions. These permit the generation of fundamentals of the same pitch, but with different percentages of upper partials, thus obtaining all the fundamentals and harmonics necessary to complete the monophonic possibilities.

Instrumental techniques will next be investigated which allow the exploitation of yet another phenomenon—the generation, at one and the same time, of a number of frequency vibrations in the single air column of an instrument. This means that woodwind can not only produce a wide variety of chords but also pass from the emission of a single sound to a group of sounds emitted together and vice versa. In this way monophonic and multiphonic possibilities can be linked in a true instrumental polyphony.

But before passing to an examination of these possibilities, we consider it useful to give an idea of the real harmonic complexity of the sound groups produced by woodwind and of the actual synthesis that the human ear can deduce from them. It must be immediately stressed that woodwind are not able to produce chords composed entirely of fundamentals, as string instruments can, for example, but groups of sounds of differing quality, which we shall therefore call sound amalgams.

The harmonic complexity of a woodwind sound amalgam can be deduced from the following audiogram of a combination of sounds produced by the oboe. This audiogram reveals that this type of sound amalgam consists of a fundamental tone and some dozens of partial tones of very varied volume.

*CHORD n. 3 initial part of sound*

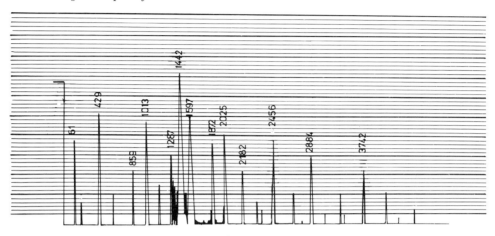

*CHORD n. 3 steady part of sound*

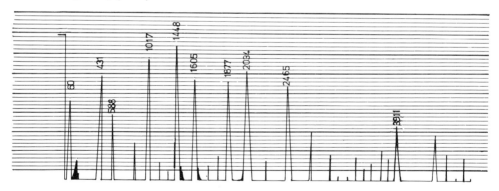

The synthesis the human ear produces from this complex sound is shown below in musical notation, the sound amalgam as written being classified aurally *before* the electronic analysis took place.

It will be seen that these notes correspond to four partial tones of some volume (431 = G♯, 588 = D natural, 1017 = B♮, and 1605 = G♮), but others, including the fundamental, remain subdued to the ear, even though in reality they are quite loud. This is why these four tones are heard, while others, including the fundamental, remain subdued to the ear. This is also why woodwind sound amalgams (though audibly comparatively simple, but in reality of a very complex nature) have such an original and fascinating timbre.

To demonstrate the above more fully, an analysis of 12 oboe sound amalgams is given below, using the following order in each case: (*a*) the Herz frequencies (i.e. vibrations per second) of the loudest sounds of sound amalgams, determined electronically: (*b*) their corresponding musical notation, and (*c*) components of the sound amalgam as deter-

mined by ear before the electronic analysis. In comparing the results of these two types of sound amalgam analysis—the one scientific (*a*) and (*b*), the other empiric (*c*)—certain small differences will be observed. These differences are of course inevitable when one compares the 'musical' impression of a voice or instrument with its electronic analysis.[1]

The objectives now aimed at are therefore those of obtaining:

(a) the linking of monophonic and multiphonic sounds;
(b) the production of homogeneous sound amalgams, in which a fundamental is accompanied by harmonics of more or less equal volume;
(c) sound amalgams which contain sounds of different timbre, the most distinctive type being that in which two sounds are emitted about a semitone apart with, in addition, their respective harmonics.

At this point we must stress most strongly that such sound phenomena are the exclusive province of woodwind instruments. It seems certain that an instrumental polyphony which includes such variety of tone colour is hardly translatable into other instrumental terms. Nevertheless it has been established that any wind instrument can be used to produce multiple sounds, adopting technical devices similar to those we have used for woodwind, and also to play music with quarter-tones having a precise pitch. Slide trombones in particular seem to offer extremely interesting possibilities, but there is no doubt that all the brass will reveal marvellous potentialities.

## A. THE LINKING OF MONOPHONIC AND MULTIPHONIC SOUNDS

Single sounds may be emitted and then joined to groups of notes in the form of sound amalgams (and vice versa) without interrupting the flow of sound and *without changing the fingering*.

Such a linking is made possible by applying the various embouchure and blowing techniques (shown on pp. 9–11) to all fingerings, though all may not produce satisfactory results. In fact, some of

---

[1] The audiograms of the analysis of the twelve sound amalgams, an example of which is shown on page 43, have been carried out at the Istituto Nazionale Elettronico of Turin directed by Prof. Gino Sacerdote.

them, even when used with different embouchures and air pressures, give no other result than the emission of a single sound.

Those fingerings which produce only single sounds may be termed 'monovalent', while those suitable for passing from single sounds to chords may be called 'polyvalent'. It is especially notable that the clarinet seems unique among woodwind instruments in that all fingerings are polyvalent, including those established by tradition.

We shall now proceed to deal with the various ways of linking single and multiple sounds. There are four possible links: from a single sound to a sound amalgam and vice versa, from the amalgam to one of its upper sounds and vice versa. For their performance the fingering remains unchanged, but the embouchure and air pressure are altered. Contrary to normal playing usage, the three performing means are here used independently of each other. In fact, one passes from the emission of a single sound to the sound amalgam by changing embouchure and increasing or decreasing air pressure, passing then from the sound amalgam to the emission of only the highest sound by simply increasing the air pressure. Naturally, this is also valid in reverse.

*Linking single sounds to sound amalgams*

From the examples in Ex. 18 it is obvious that lip and breath control are of paramount importance. [In fact, slight modifications of embouchure, lip pressure, and air pressure are such determining factors in the formation of these new sounds that it can be stated categorically that no satisfactory results can be obtained until the performer has acquired a considerable sensitivity of embouchure and breath control and is able to modify these at will, without hesitation and with complete accuracy. Unfortunately, it is quite impossible to state precisely how each embouchure should be formed. Different players have, by nature, lips of varying thickness and formation, so no two players use exactly the same embouchure for any given sound. Further, the embouchure requirements of this new technique can hardly be formulated in words, for they are achieved more by the 'feel' of the lip on the reed than by taking just so many millimetres

Ex. 18.

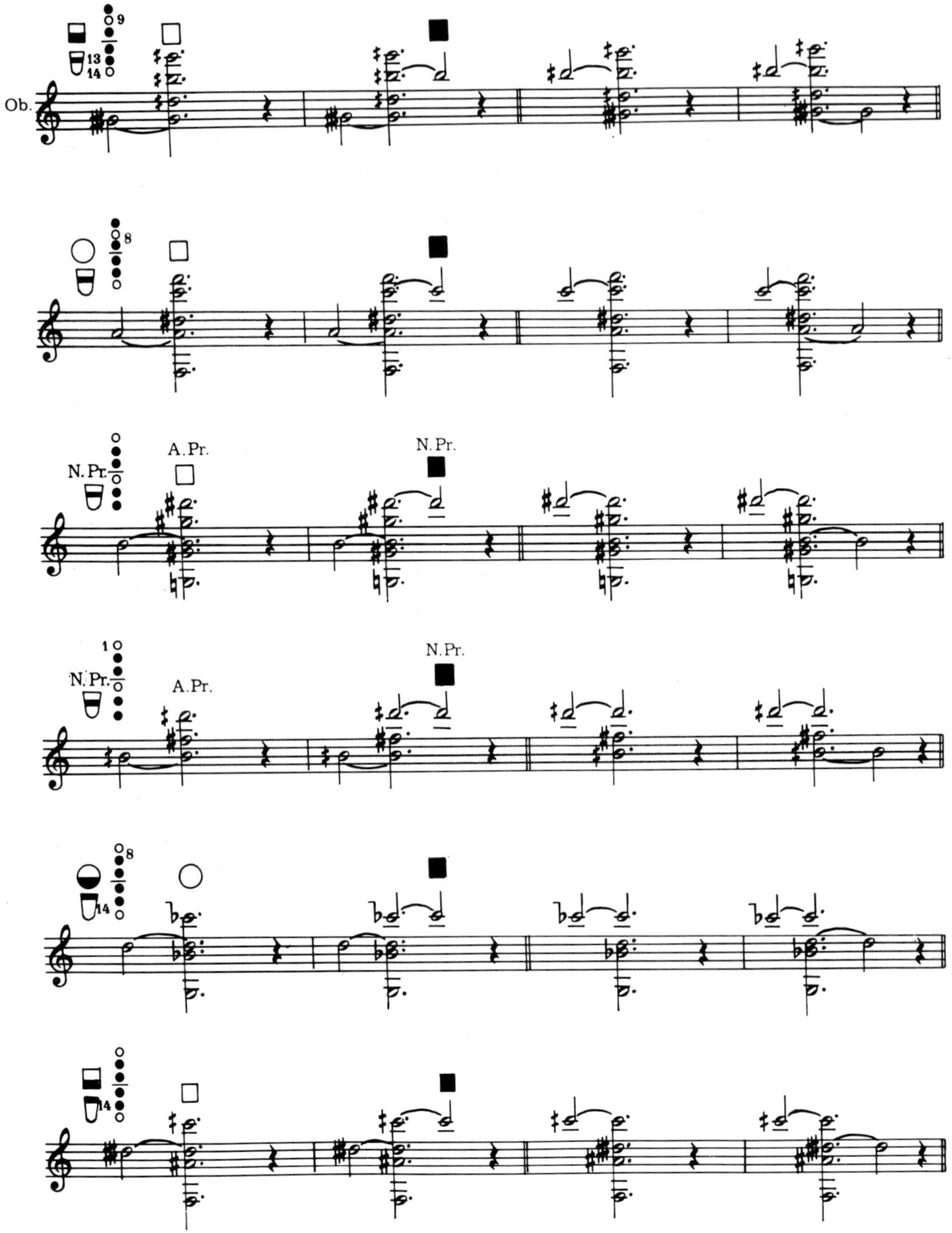
Ob.
N. Pr.
A. Pr.
N. Pr.
N. Pr.
A. Pr.
N. Pr.

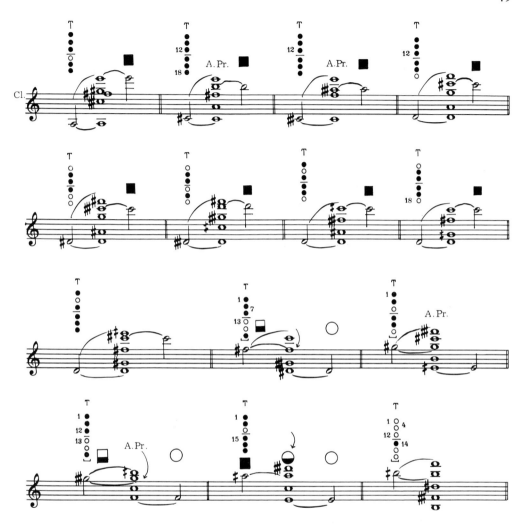

of reed. In short, the player must discover the lip sensations for each type of sound for himself and learn to use just the right lip and air pressure required in any given situation. The indications of embouchure and air pressure given in the examples are therefore, at best, only approximate. (Ed.)]

In the previous examples some fingerings are the same as those which have already been used to form fundamentals and their relative harmonics. This is done in order to show that in the production of sound amalgams some harmonics are brought out which are different from those which occurred previously, when we were only concerned with the emission of single sounds.

We will now pass on to demonstrate how sound amalgams can be emitted directly, without any preparation.

### B. HOMOGENEOUS SOUND AMALGAMS

These may contain up to five or six sounds, their main characteristic being that all sounds are of approximately the same volume and tone colour, that is, of the type shown as nos. 3 and 10 in the analyses of the twelve sound amalgams (p. 44); this is very different from the type we shall present in the next section.

We have already seen how it is possible to attack sound amalgams directly in illustrating the linking of a sound amalgam to a single sound and therefore the technique described above can be used (see Ex. 18, p. 47).

Another means of producing homogeneous sound amalgams is given by a type of fingering which may be called multiphonic, in that the initial result—obtained with a *normal reed position*—is the emission of a group of sounds. This is true also for the flute, for no alteration in lip position is needed. It is quite easy to discover multiphonic fingerings: using a normal reed position, the player chooses any fingering suitable for the emission of a fundamental tone and then, by opening or closing one or more holes (either finger holes or holes closed by chromatic keys) he will discover that certain fingerings produce chords. After these have been notated and classified, they can be used when desired and in any suitable order.

In providing several examples of homogeneous sound amalgams and successions of such sound amalgams, only the fingerings will be given and no reed position and special lip and air pressure indicated unless these are necessary (as with certain sound amalgams for the reed instruments). Where only fingerings are given, this means that embouchures, lip and air pressures are normal, or that the divergence from standard playing methods is minimal. The player may have to make slight adjustments which he must learn by experience, just as experience has already taught him how to adjust his lips and increase or decrease the air pressure in order to change register effectively.

Ex. 19. *Homogeneous sound amalgams*

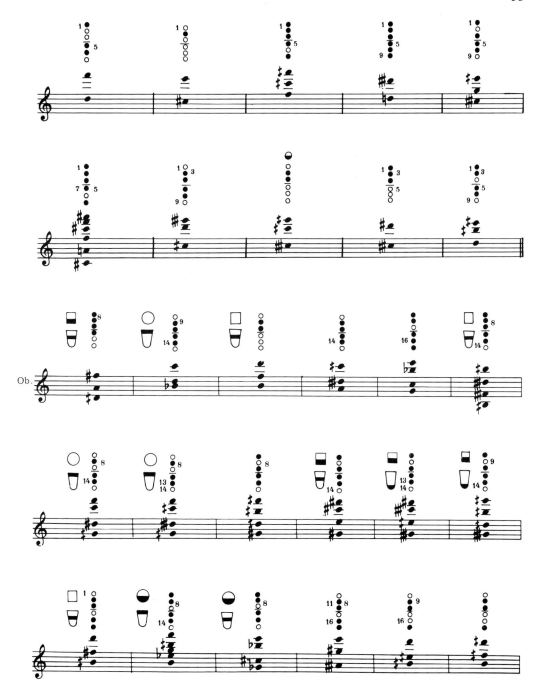

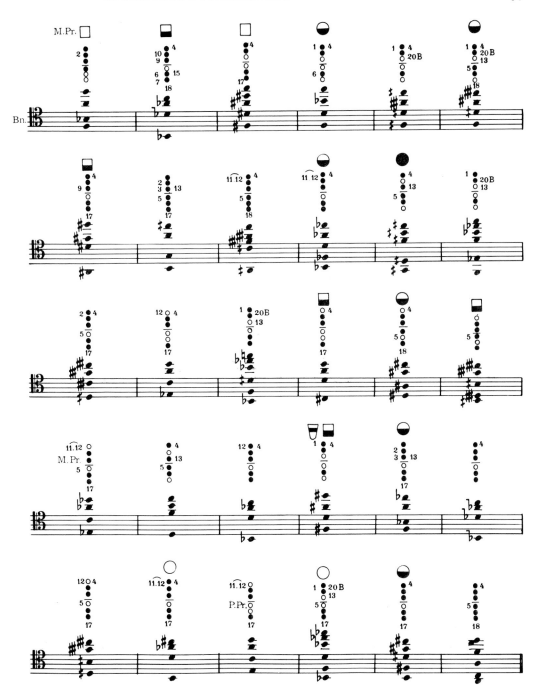

Homogeneous sound amalgams can generally be put together in any harmonic sequence, and we give some examples particularly to show the interesting independent movement of the parts that can be produced in each sequence.

Ex. 20. *Successions of homogeneous sound amalgams*

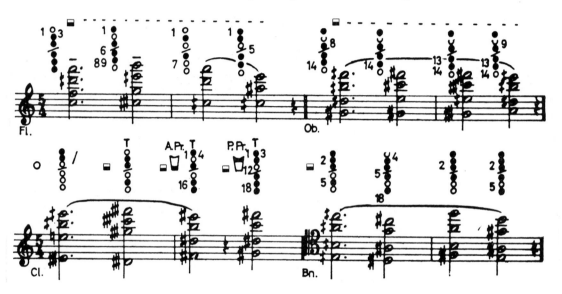

But this is not all, for multiphonic fingerings can be made to produce (though not always) three different sound amalgams—the first with the normal reed position, the second using more reed than usual and the third moving towards the tip of the reed. The three sound amalgams can be played either separately or linked together by changing the embouchure and reducing or increasing the air pressure as necessary. In this way it is possible to play sound amalgams of great effect without excessive difficulty.

[1] (*See facing page*) If all components (fundamentals and harmonics) of a broken sound were indicated on the music stave, there would inevitably be an excessive complication in notation which would only lead to confusion. For this reason broken sounds are indicated by a single symbol—the square note indicating that sound which is most prominent and of the most characteristic tone colour.

Ex. 21. *Three sound amalgams from one fingering*

C. SOUND AMALGAMS CONTAINING SOUNDS OF DIFFERENT TIMBRE

The homogeneous sound amalgams just described frequently contain sounds of different tone colour. Some sounds may be relatively dull and others bright, but these differences are not clearly evident. The sound amalgams now to be described contain sounds of such sharply contrasting colour that the effect is immediately recognizable as being altogether different from homogeneous sound amalgams.

As has already been briefly mentioned, sound amalgams containing sounds of different tone colour are obtained by emitting simultaneously two sounds which are close together, with their relative harmonics. In this way it is possible to exploit the phenomenon of 'beats' caused by the interference in sound vibrations occurring when two sounds are emitted which are very close together, within the maximum space of a semitone. This type of sound amalgam is shown as no. 4 in the electronic analysis (p. 44). In addition, we can use a harmonic and a sound which, because of its strong beats caused by the partial interference with its vibrations, has such a strongly characteristic tone colour that it is unmistakable. It is accurately described by the term *broken sound*, and in these examples is indicated by a square note, thus—■.[1]

It would seem that in a broken sound one note is continuous while the other is broken and therefore becomes more in evidence. It is to be noted that each of the two sounds in the various combinations above mentioned can be emitted individually and then linked with the other. In this way it is possible to create polyphonic passages of extraordinary subtlety, given the noticeably different tone colour of the two voices. As there is nothing new to observe as to the performing technique needed for such passages, we can move on immediately to a number of examples which illustrate various possibilities:

In Ex. 22 are shown:
At (a) *Linking a harmonic to a broken sound*
At (b) *Linking a harmonic to a broken sound and returning to the harmonic*
At (c) *The two sounds emitted together*
At (d) *The two sounds emitted together, followed by a single harmonic*
At (e) *The two sounds emitted together, followed by a single harmonic and then returning to the two sounds*

Ex. 22.

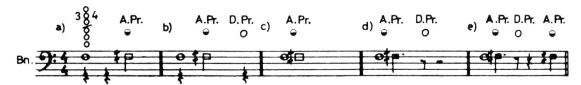

The next examples illustrate another phenomenon—the emission of two sounds of the same pitch in *unison*. The effect is quite noticeable, as the two sounds have quite different tonal spectra. One is dull, lacking in overtones, while the other is bright with prominent upper partials. The effect is of a true unison of two sounds of the same pitch, but of different character. As will be seen from the following examples, the change from a single sound to a unison of two sounds of the same pitch is accomplished with the reed instruments by changes in fingerings. In the case of the flute, the 'second' sound forming a unison with the first is obtained by using the lip apertures indicated, and not by changing fingerings as with the other instruments.

In Ex. 23 are shown:

At (a) *A harmonic joined to another harmonic of the same pitch*

At (b) *A harmonic linked to another harmonic and a return to the first harmonic*

At (c) *The two sounds emitted together as a unison*

At (d) *Two harmonics emitted together followed by a single harmonic*

At (e) *Two harmonics emitted together, followed by a single harmonic and then a return to the unison*

Ex. 23.

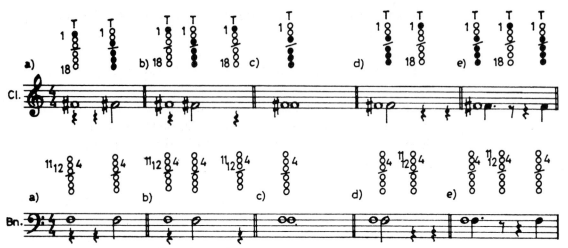

Sound amalgams will now be examined which are obtained by making use of another phenomenon in direct relationship with that of beats—differential tones (the so-called Tartini's 'third sounds').[1] It is possible to obtain differential tones which are *lower* than the notes of a chord when the interval between the lower notes of such a chord does not exceed an octave. Sometimes the differential

[1] Differential tones belong to the class of combination or resultant tones. If two loud notes are sounded together they create a third and fourth sound, one below (differential tone) and the other above the original sounds (summational tone). Differential tones are the most important type, as they are audibly more evident, the name being derived from the fact that the frequency of a differential tone is equal to the *difference* between the vibration frequencies of the two generating notes. Thus if two generating notes are very close together, the difference between their vibration numbers will be small and the differential tone will therefore be of low frequency, below the normal compass of an instrument. This probably accounts for the very disturbed quality of 'broken' sounds formed by sounding simultaneously two notes which are very close together. As the difference in frequency between the two generating sounds increases, so will the differential tone rise in pitch, and, in fact, becomes less audible.

As for summational tones, these have frequencies equal to the *sum* of the vibration numbers of the two generators and therefore summational tones are higher in pitch than the generators. However, they are much less audible than differential tones and are considered to be less important. Other combination tones exist, but have much less influence on sound sensations and therefore need not be discussed here.

Books on acoustics usually stress that differential tones are only produced if the generators are of loud volume and perfectly in tune, so it is probable that players will be able to produce these tones only when the main notes of a chord are played at adequate volume and with exact pitch. (Ed.)

tone is formed *below the normal compass of instruments*.[1] Alternatively, differential tones can be formed between two sounds if these are more than an octave apart.

The tone colour of such chords is truly unusual and quite fascinating, especially so in cases where chords comprise harmonics, broken sounds, and differential tones. These latter, however, are not always of sufficient volume as to justify their inclusion in the notation. Nevertheless, they can contribute in a most effective way to certain subtle colouristic effects.

Ex. 24. *Sound amalgams with sounds of different tone colour including a differential tone and a broken sound*

[1] This type of sound amalgam is shown as no. 8 etc in the electronic analysis. (p. 44).

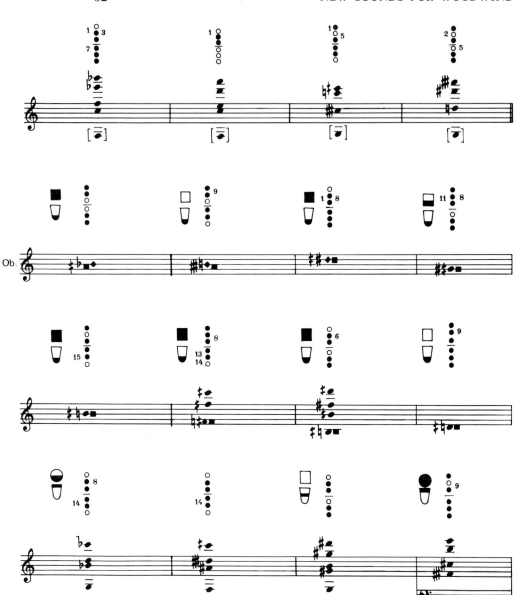

Many different harmonic sequences can also be obtained with this type of sound amalgam. It must, however, be noted that sound amalgams with broken sounds sometimes by their very nature do not link together easily, and it is advisable in this case to consult an instrumentalist who can check on their smooth performance.

Ex. 25. *Successions of sound amalgams of the same type as in the previous example*

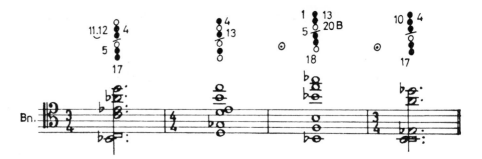

To conclude the examination of multiphonic possibilities, particular mention must be made of one special type of fingering which produces results of such an unpredictable nature that they are by no means easy to classify. Any of these fingerings can produce various homogeneous chords and also chords containing sounds of different tone colour. In addition, a variety of single sounds can be played which can serve to link the various chords together. To obtain such passages, the performer only needs to increase or decrease the air pressure while passing through the various reed positions, without altering the fingering. Such fingerings give results which are as varied as they are unpredictable and because of the 'chance' element in their use we will call them 'aleatory fingerings'.[1]

Woodwind instruments therefore possess an inherent quality which fits in unusually well with the spirit underlying the conception of aleatory music. Using more than one aleatory fingering, we have at our disposal a large quantity of sound results which cannot possibly be set in any specific order and therefore demand a musical conception which is not organized. This is surely a unique situation, providing perfect conditions for that close collaboration between composer and performer which is so indispensable for the realization of music notated only in a schematic design and not on the well-defined music stave.

To be consistent with the spirit of such music, we will therefore limit ourselves to providing a number of aleatory fingerings for each

[1] 'Aleatory' is derived from the Latin 'alea', a game of dice, in which the chance element is predominant. 'Aleatory' music, in fact, deliberately cultivates the unpredictable, the composer preferring sound results which are thrown out by accident rather than by his own design. (Ed.)

instrument, sufficient for playing a short piece of music, without
notating any specific sound results. We will leave the realization of
such results to the performer, for to indicate any music in notation
would not only be quite contrary to the purpose and use of these
fingerings, but would be a negation of the spirit of aleatory music. In
any case, the player must build up his own individual knowledge and
musical experience. This latter is so subjective that he cannot benefit
from the experience of others.

It must be remembered that in performing such a piece of music the
performer must also bring into use all those expressive and colouristic
effects which have already been discussed earlier in this book, as and
when they are needed. To use aleatory fingerings without moulding
the sound results (however unexpected they may be) into an expressive sequence of events would make for music which has neither
significance nor interest.

Ex. 26. *Aleatory fingerings*

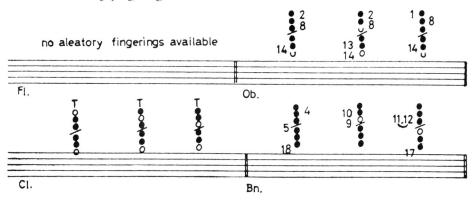

# 4 monophonic and multiphonic possibilities combined

It is proper that this chapter should begin with a gesture of homage to Arnold Schoenberg and in particular to one of his most fruitful discoveries, the melody of tone colours, about which he wrote in his *Harmonielehre*: 'I am not inclined to admit without reservation that difference between the timbre and pitch of sounds of which we usually speak. I think rather that sound makes itself evident through timbre, of which pitch is one dimension. Timbre is therefore the complete whole, whereas pitch is only a part of this whole, or rather, pitch is only timbre measured in a single direction. Now if it is possible to use timbres which are distinguished one from another by pitch so as to create structures which we call melodies (successions of sounds which by their relationship with each other give the impression of a logical discourse) then it must also be possible, using the timbres of the other dimension, those we simply call "timbre", to construct sound successions whose interrelationship has the effect of a kind of logic, completely equivalent to the kind of logic which satisfies us in melodies made through pitch.'

It would appear that what to Schoenberg seemed a 'fantasy of the future' is now quite within the capabilities of each woodwind instrument. We have already seen how each instrument can emit the same sound with tone colours of notably different character, and in addition certain unison effects can be obtained which can contribute in a subtle way to the timbric transformation of the single sound (Exx. 23a–23e). These resources in tone colour are obviously rich enough to select say, a dozen most characteristic timbres with which to form sound successions which by their mutual rapport create a logic equivalent to that which satisfies us in melodies made only through pitch.

When it is considered that, in addition, there are many ways of transforming the tone colour of sounds (variations in lip pressure, oscillations, vibrato, the 'smorzato', etc.) it should be evident that woodwind instruments have quite a rich vocabulary with which to create Schoenberg's 'timbres of the other dimension' through the medium of a single instrument. As an example of the refinement of effect which is possible, we quote a portion of the author's *Concertazioni* for oboe and several instruments:

Ex. 27.

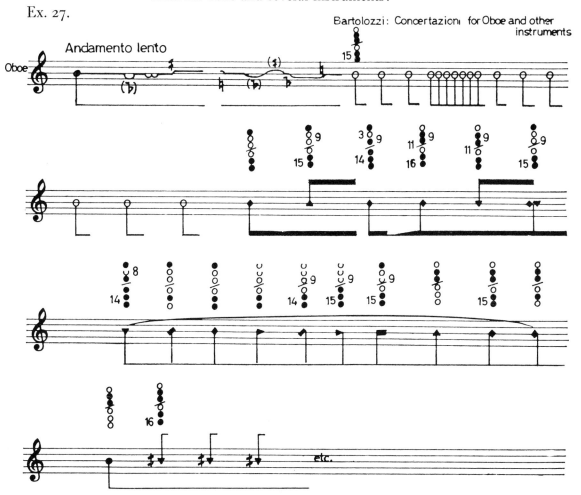

(Copyright Ediz. Suvini Zerboni, Milan)

[The notation used in the above example is not of traditional type. This notation, used again on pp. 104–13 for music illustrated on the accompanying disc, will be more fully explained on p. 103. For the moment it is sufficient to say that the duration of notes is in proportion to the length of the horizontal line attached to the stem of each note and that the volume is indicated by the thickness of this line. Variously shaped notes are used by the composer in *Concertazioni* to indicate different tone colours. (Ed.)]

SPECIAL MULTIPHONIC EFFECTS

*Multiple trills*
The performance of multiple trills between two sound amalgams does not present any particular difficulty. It is sufficient to open and close one or more finger and/or key holes rapidly and the player can pass from one initial sound amalgam to another with extreme agility. The finger or key holes used for the trill may be among those used in the fingering of the first sound amalgam or may be among those remaining free. Sometimes one or more of the notes of the first sound amalgam remain unaltered and sound uninterruptedly in both sound amalgams while the remaining notes trill between themselves. In this way it is possible to play virtuoso-sounding passages of great effect throughout the entire compass of intensity from *pp* to *ff*.

Ex. 28.

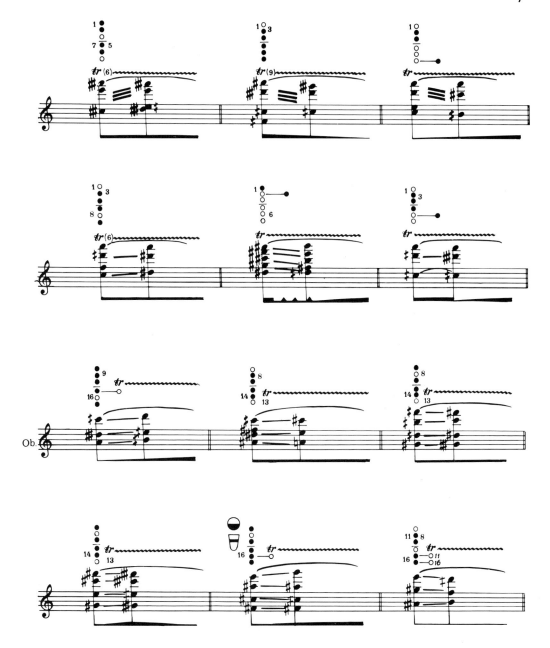

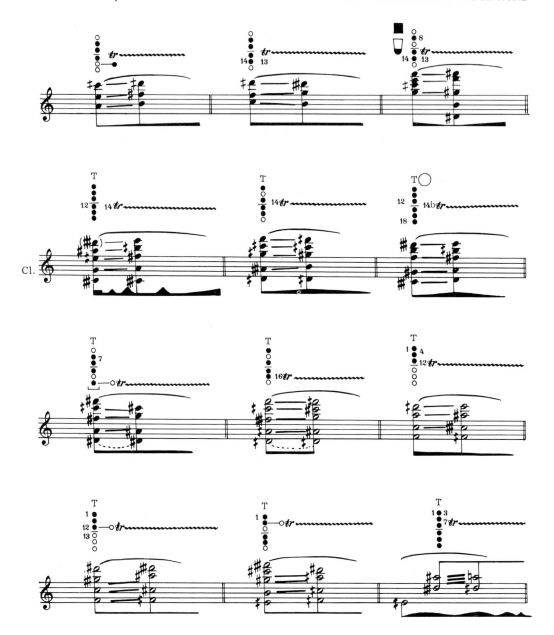

It may be noted in passing that multiple trills offer a striking example of how new chordal combinations can be so easily discovered by the simple opening and closing of holes in any given fingering which already produces a known sound amalgam.

### 'Smorzato' effects with sound amalgams

The chordal 'smorzato' is produced in the same way as that for single sounds. It will be found, however, that a relatively small number of sound amalgams do not lend themselves to this effect. The chordal 'smorzato' is indicated as follows:

Ex. 29.

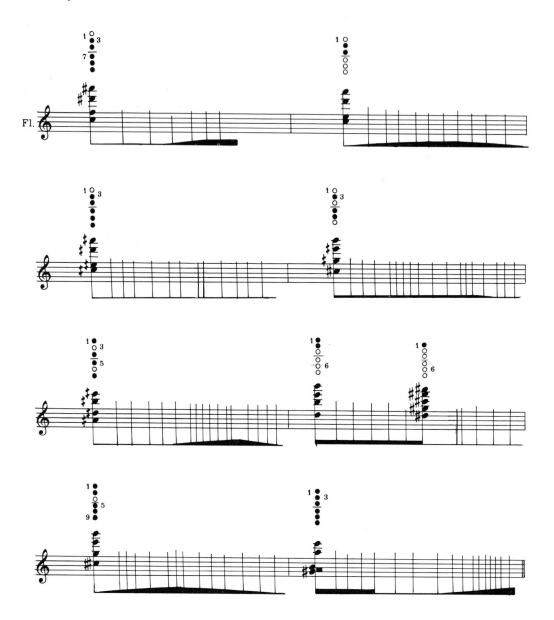

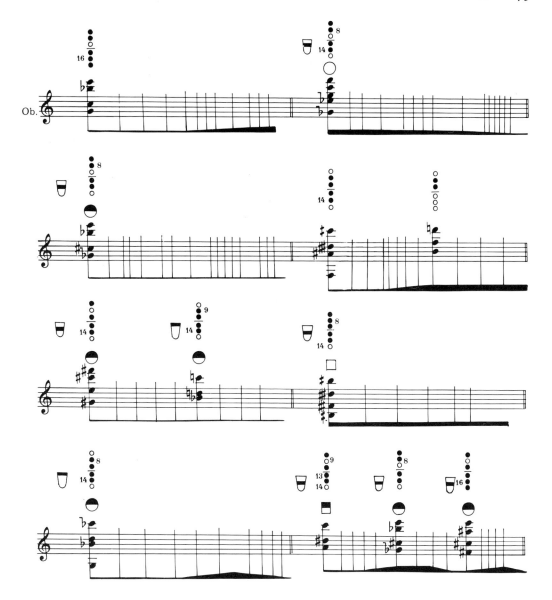

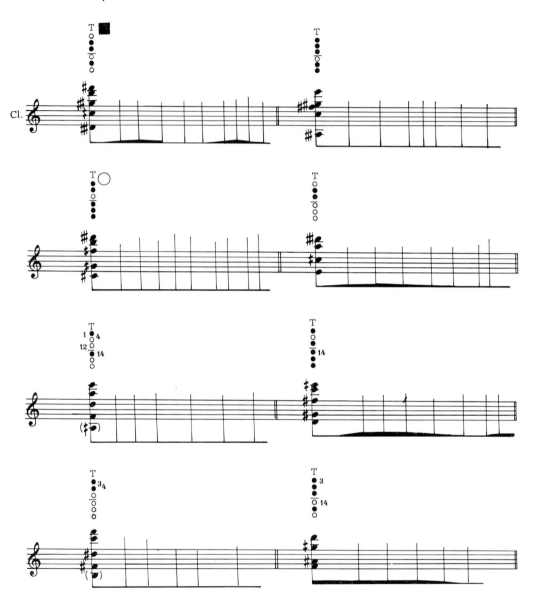

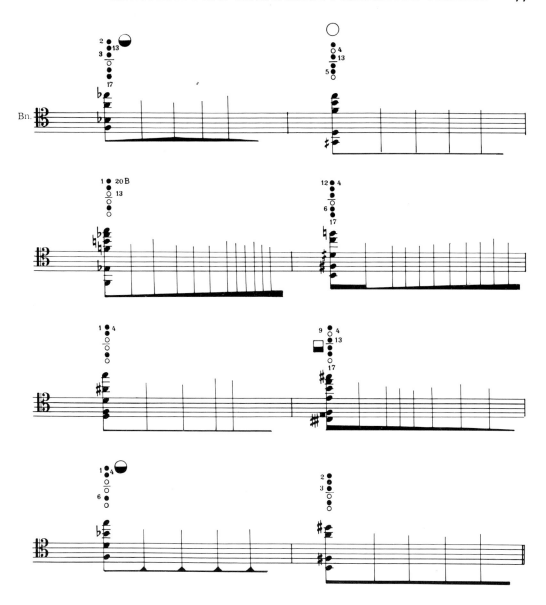

Another way of using 'smorzato' is given by some sound amalgams in which certain sounds can be maintained throughout, while other sounds of the same sound amalgam can be suppressed at any given moment and with any desired rhythm. For example:

Ex. 30. *'Smorzato' sound amalgams superimposed rhythmically on a
single continuous sound*

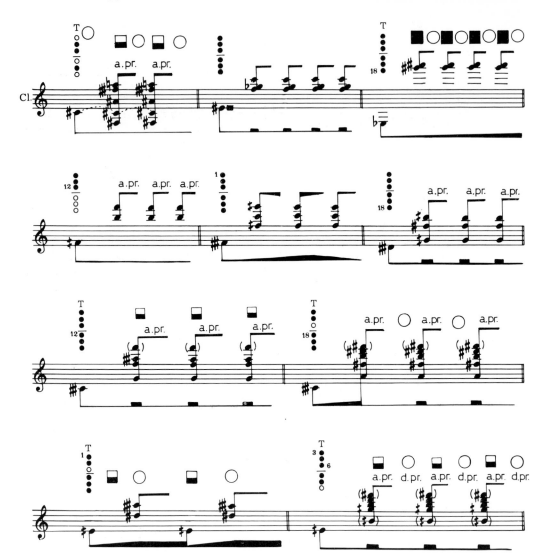

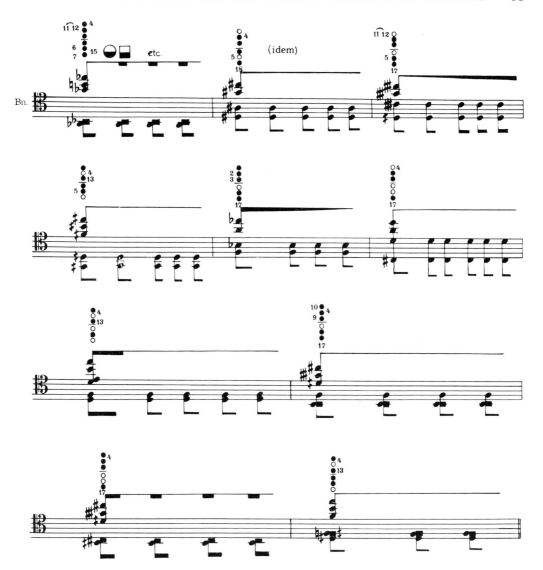

In Ex. 30 the *lower* notes are sustained in the flute, oboe, and clarinet, while with the bassoon, the *upper* notes are held continuously. The 'smorzato' sounds are interrupted or 'choked off' when lip pressure is relaxed (by lowering the jaw) and sound again when pressure is increased once more. The continuous sounds are not altered by the changes in lip pressure. In the case of the flute, this effect is produced by beginning with a slightly reduced aperture (▬) and then enlarging the lip opening slightly to produce the 'smorzato' of only the higher notes.

*Single sounds with the rhythmical superimposition of another sound*
This is produced by holding the single sounds without interruption and superimposing the other sound by a rapid movement of the finger which operates the appropriate key or hole. If the movement is not perfectly synchronized the single sound may be interrupted. In the case of the flute, it is produced by holding the single sound without interruption and increasing the air pressure whenever it is desired momentarily to superimpose the other sound. This is a very striking effect which should be used with a dynamic level not exceeding *mp*.

Ex. 31.

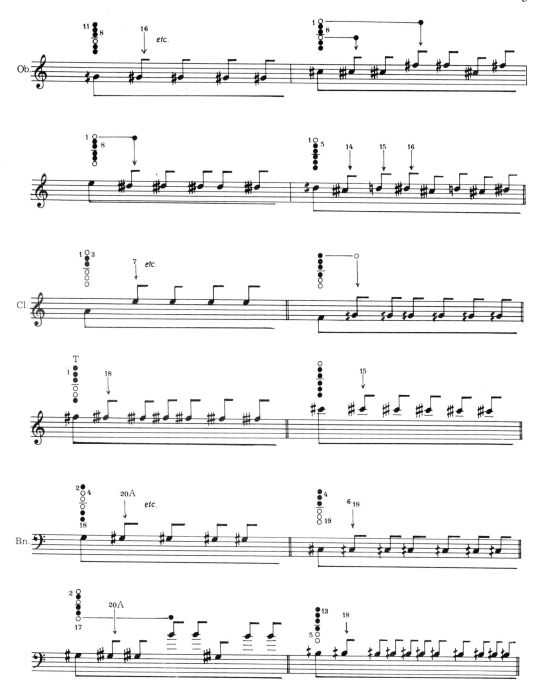

*Trilled sound with rhythmic superimposition of another sound*
The performance is similar to that of the preceding effect, except
that the held note is trilled instead of being steady.

Ex. 32.

*Trills between two sound amalgams combined with the simultaneous per-
formance of other sounds foreign to the amalgams themselves*

The performance is similar to that used for trills between two sound
amalgams with the addition of the simultaneous operation of holes
or keys not required for the two fingerings. In this way, while the
trills continue without interruption, other sounds can be produced
in any desired rhythm. Naturally this is possible only when the
combination of fingerings permits.

Ex. 33.

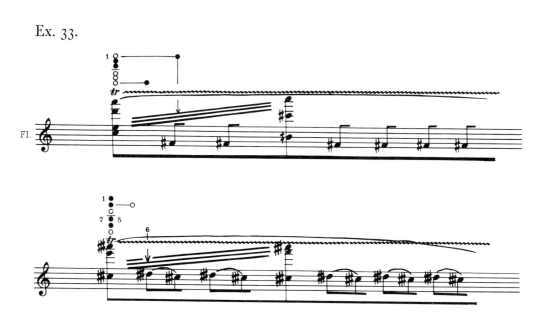

*Glissando between two sound amalgams*

As this effect requires a different technique according to the instrument used, we shall illustrate its performance separately:

FLUTE It does not appear that any kind of multiphonic glissando is possible.

OBOE Both ascending and descending multiphonic glissandi can be obtained by moving from the normal reed position to the upper or lower position and increasing or diminishing the air pressure as necessary. Because of its aleatory nature it is preferable not to indicate the terminal point of the glissando.

Ex. 34.

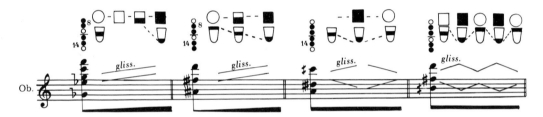

CLARINET Ascending glissandi are obtained by gradually increasing the air and lip pressure and by sliding as necessary the fingers engaged in opening one or more holes, as is shown by the dotted lines between the two fingerings. It is apparently not possible to produce any descending multiphonic glissandi. The long glissando can be performed beginning and ending at any point between the two limits.

Ex. 35.

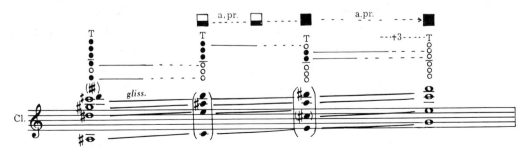

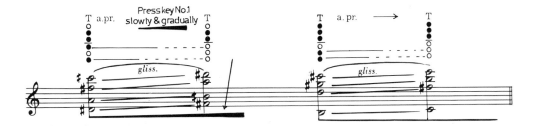

BASSOON It is only possible to obtain descending glissandi with a crescendo from *p* to *fff*. This is a very striking instrumental effect because of the extremely powerful sound that can be produced. The terminal point of the glissando is always aleatory and it can be obtained also with distortion of the lower sounds.

Ex. 36.

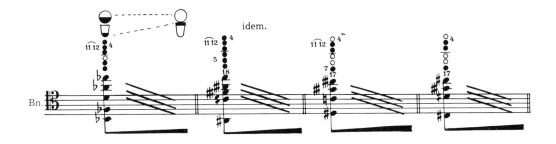

To conclude the explanation of the various techniques which have been presented up to now, mention must be made of some points which should be helpful in mastering the various monophonic and multiphonic effects. It must be stressed that even the most detailed technical description or indication may not be equally valid for every player or instrument. For them to have absolute validity we would have to achieve the impossible. Every player would need to have identical physical characteristics. Every instrument and reed would have to be precisely similar. Inevitably, different results are to be expected, mostly through variety in the shape of players' lips, different reeds, mouthpieces, crooks, barrels, etc.

But this is in the natural order of things and should not be too much regarded. In fact, it is only necessary to modify those performing indications which do not correspond exactly with the player's physical characteristics or his instrument, in order to obtain good results. These modifications will usually be no more than slight adjustments of the embouchure or wind pressure. Certainly no alteration of fingerings need be considered.

The reed must be prepared with extreme care. It has to function in an unusual way, and this is a decisive factor in the production of these new sounds. To remove any doubts on this matter, it can be affirmed that if a reed works well and is perfectly suited to normal usage, it is also completely suitable for all technical needs. If a player finds any difference in results between one reed and another, this is easily corrected by small adjustments in embouchure, lip pressure or air pressure. The use of more than one reed in a performance is not advisable, nor is it necessary.

It is hoped that players will understand most clearly that if they intend to dedicate themselves to mastering these new techniques they must free themselves for the moment from the rules of traditional instrumental usage. This usage has most excellent and indispensable qualities, but it only lends itself to perfection, not to fruitful development. The player must regard his instrument as a means which, far from having reached its limit of expression, has great resources which have yet to be exploited. This will become a natural outlook to those who, in the future, can be initiated from the beginning of their studies in the new techniques which, being nothing other than a consequential development of traditional ones, can only be of benefit to performers.

It remains to be seen how this conviction will spread, and how slow preconceptions and ingrained habits will be to die. Probably such prejudices will disappear in direct proportion to the interest these new sound phenomena will awaken in composers—that is, in proportion to the suitability of these instrumental developments to the needs of contemporary music.

We will conclude this chapter with a complete list of all the instrumental possibilities we have dealt with, so that a full picture of them can be presented:

A. The unification of the intonation of the natural scale throughout the entire compass of instruments.

B. The possibility of emitting the same sound with timbres of considerable diversity, thus permitting the performance of melodies of tone colour with either a single sound, or sounds of different pitch.

C. The possibility of emitting homogeneous sound amalgams and therefore of being able to organize, among other things, successions of amalgams with independent movement of each voice part.

D. The possibility of emitting sound amalgams containing sounds of different tone colour, that is, sound amalgams which comprise up to three different kinds of sounds—harmonics, broken sounds, and differential tones.

E. The unification of monophonic and multiphonic possibilities (through linking sounds, passing from single sounds to sound amalgams and vice versa) to give a completely effective polyphonic movement.

F. The emission of quarter-tones throughout the compass of instruments, thus amplifying melodic resources.

G. The emission of sound amalgams containing quarter-tones, thus augmenting harmonic resources.

On pages 104–13 will be found music examples which have been recorded on the disc which accompanies this publication, and which are intended as an illustration of the main technical possibilities of each instrument. Inevitably some sacrifice of musical logic has had to be made in order to illustrate, in a kind of 'collage', the various instrumental resources within such a short period of time.

# 5 *final observations*

In conclusion, there are a few comments which must be made in order to facilitate the introduction of these new woodwind sounds into common compositional practice.

It will have been noticed that though it has been possible to demonstrate in theory how to exploit the various new techniques, no indication has been given of how fingerings and embouchures, etc., can be preselected (apart, naturally, from those already known). If a composer wants a certain combination of sounds, it is impossible to predict what fingering will be necessary, unless this has already been discovered. Vice versa, the sounds which will be produced from any uninvestigated fingering are quite unpredictable and even where sounds produced by one embouchure are known, it is impossible to guess what happens if the embouchure, lip or air pressure is altered. This may seem a grave defect, but it is not so serious as would at first appear. On the contrary, it may be regarded as a necessary obstacle, for it prevents composers writing in the abstract, without any real experience of these sound phenomena. Even if composers did have a theoretical way of working, they could never foresee the exact timbric result of any sound combination—and this is the essential factor. Only listening can give this knowledge. Tone colours are so unpredictable. Single sounds, or even a simple triad, can gain a new purity, so that the most hackneyed phrase may be heard as something fresh and new.

This need of auditory experience is even more vital when writing music which involves the use of quarter-tones, whether they are used as melody or in chords.

It is therefore essential that a composer does not work in the abstract, but in close collaboration with a performer, until he is completely familiar with the sound material he wishes to use. When this is impossible, he will have to learn what he can from the recording made available with this publication. This is not an ideal solution, but at least he will learn a fair vocabulary of effects.

The evolution of instrumental music has always been brought about by reciprocal collaboration between composers and performers, so the statement that composers should avoid working in a vacuum is neither new nor unusual. It has always been an essential condition for every real evolution of instrumental music. That composers and performers have sometimes in the past been one and the same person does not alter the problem in the least. Indeed, it would be more to the point if we asked ourselves just how much certain limitations in the development of woodwind technique do not depend directly on the fact that no composer-performer has ever done for woodwind what Paganini, Liszt, and Busoni did for their own instruments. The fact remains that true instrumental conquests have never been the fruit of abstract conceptions, but of toilsome direct experience. The recent exceptional development of percussion instruments illustrates that a whole section of the orchestra, relegated previously to tasks of an elementary nature, has in a brief time assumed a role of first importance in contemporary music.

Another matter which presents some difficulty is the classification and notation of sound material—a work which needs great care and attention if the pitch and timbre of sounds is to be correctly ascertained. This can best be done with an electronic sound spectrograph, but as this will not normally be available, the best method is for the composer to work with the performer, using a second instrument to identify sounds. It is difficult for a player to do this work alone, for he would have to interrupt constantly the emission of a sound or chord to confirm the pitch of the various notes. Instead, two persons can work quickly; one emits the sound continuously, the other tests the pitch of the various components and writes them down together with details of fingering, embouchure, etc. Because of its imperfect intonation, a piano is unsuitable for this work. A string instrument has been found to be far preferable. In order to determine the sounds of a chord, it is best to establish the pitch of one sound first, in order to have a point of reference, and then through this the pitch of the other sounds can be found. The lowest sound should not be used, especially those differential tones which are below the normal compass of an instrument, as these are usually the last to be brought out with adequate volume, and can only be made well evident after much practice. Naturally in the case of chords with sounds of different tone colour derived from two notes close together the point of reference for pitch will be the two notes themselves.

In the case of polyphonic fingerings (which can produce more than one chord for each fingering through the use of different embouchures and varied lip and air pressure), it is best to establish first which chord is produced by the most normal embouchure and blowing technique, passing then to the notation of those chords which need more and more divergence from normal embouchures, etc. As each chord is notated, it is then possible to find which single sounds can be produced with the same embouchure, but with varied air and lip pressure. Such a rational procedure will rapidly provide full information of the complete resources of polyphonic fingerings, and will illustrate how a minimum of fingerings, used with intelligence, can give a notable quantity of sound results.

As soon as the performer has achieved some facility in producing the new sounds, it will be possible to move rapidly. The course of investigations will cease to be haphazard and will proceed instead by as association of events. Each new fingering will suggest a chain of possibilities, at which point the chief difficulty will not be one of finding sound material, but of classifying and notating it adequately and quickly.

Through the discovery that woodwind instruments can emit the same sound with well-differentiated tone colours, they can now enter into a new phase of orchestral use. These instruments, first used in the orchestra to double string parts and later relegated by the early classic composers to a humble role of sustaining the harmony through holding-notes, only acquired individuality through being used in solo passages. The instrument used for solo work was chosen by the composer because of its general tone colour or 'character'. The discovery of 'registers' later opened up the second phase in the orchestral use of woodwind tone colour, and thus extends as far as those modern orchestration techniques which exploit the particular timbres natural to each register of the woodwind—low register, medium, upper, extreme high register, etc. We can now pass to a third phase through the use of a number of timbres for each sound. As modern orchestration tends to give more and more value to each individual sound, particularly through contrast in tone colour, it is evident that woodwind can now play a more vital role than ever before. This amplification of the colouristic resources of woodwind will make for a notable enrichment of the orchestrator's palette of tone colours, allowing a more subtle and varied play of instrumentation.

Now that different timbres are available for each note of the quarter-tone range it is possible to combine mixtures of sound of extraordinary timbric richness—for instance, a harmonic combination in which each sound changes timbre several times in the course of its duration, or else the same harmonic and timbric combination broken into its individual sounds by little smorzati, or kept steady in some sounds and turned into smorzati in others, and so on. Alternatively, other mixtures of tone colours of differing quality can be obtained using the various methods of modifying the sounds by lip and breath control which we have illustrated—for example, a harmonic cluster in which each sound is made to fluctuate by means of oscillations and half-oscillations, or the same harmonic combination in which some sounds are made to fluctuate and others are kept steady, and then given a vibrato gradually increasing to a maximum of vibratissimo. All these mixtures of tone colours, and many others that can be derived from them, can produce exceedingly fascinating effects—conglomerations of sounds with unpredictable internal movement, bands of sounds with a thin veiled tone quality, tone clusters of dense and vital effect, etc.

But though these new colouristic possibilities for single sounds will be important in enriching the orchestral colour spectrum, they can hardly compare with the new resources of timbre offered by multiphonic effects, resources which, together with the monophonic effects, are so ample as to disrupt any conventional scheme of orchestration. In fact it is not easy to assess the consequences of introducing the vast quantity of new woodwind sounds into the orchestra, because the usual principles of instrumental usage will no longer be valid.

We are faced with sound material which is very special both as regards the quality and the quantity of sounds, material which needs to be elaborated with a skill and dexterity equal to the task of organizing such new woodwind possibilities.

The last technical aspect to which we would like to call particular attention is the emission of quarter-tones, obtained no longer by the approximate method of variations in lip pressure, but by the accurate means of determined fingerings. The suitability of woodwind for playing music in quarter-tones is, however, still governed by their structure, which is not designed specifically for such purpose, and obviously there are some limitations. In fact, apart from those we have already mentioned—the slight limitations at the beginning of the quarter-tone range and the lack of three fingerings in the lower register of the modern flute with finger plates (see Ex. 7)—we must point out two other problems which have been encountered by some instrumentalists: the difficulty of playing certain intervals in tune, because the given fingerings do not produce the desired result, and the difficulty found in playing certain fast passages because the changes of fingering are by no means easy. These are two important considerations which we must attempt to answer. The first problem is not difficult to solve, as in the event of variations of intonation due to the unsuitability of the fingering, recourse can be had to the numerous alternatives available for each quarter-tone in the certainty of finding a suitable fingering. Fortunately we can point out that these alternatives are largely to be found in the existing manuals[1] and the problem is reduced to the choice of an appropriate fingering.

The solution of the second problem however, is not so easy, because sometimes excessive difficulty is created in the changes of fingering, which makes the execution of rapid quarter-tone passages almost impossible. We therefore suggest that the composer should avoid writing such passages without the agreement of an instrumentalist as to whether they can be played. If they are easy, it is worth writing them. Otherwise it is preferable to forgo such passages, bearing in

---

[1] See the *General Table of Fingerings* in the tutors already referred to, where at least ten fingerings are shown for each sound of the quarter-tone range, with the exception of the lower fundamentals which have fewer.

mind, as is well-known, that speed nullifies the distinction between a rapid succession of semitones and a similar succession of quarter-tones, even though the difference in intervals can certainly exist. Personally I have long abandoned the idea of writing such passages, having observed at first hand that there is in practice no perceptible difference between a fast passage in quarter-tones and a similar one in semitones which is much easier to perform and gives a much better virtuoso effect. The difference of the intervals is clearly perceptible as soon as we reduce the speed of performance, not only because their intonation becomes clear but also because the interesting timbric results produced by the mixture of fingerings is of notable effect.

We have drawn attention to limitations and difficulties which would certainly not be found in instruments constructed specifically to play quarter-tone music. But if we consider that despite this we can nevertheless produce a complete vocabulary of quarter-tone sounds, both monophonic and multiphonic, we can see no justification for not doing today, even with some extra difficulty, what may possibly be done more easily tomorrow. An added reason is that, with the inclusion of the complete woodwind section, the whole orchestra is capable of playing quarter-tone music, with the exception of some readily identifiable keyboard instruments. In fact it is well known that strings can play quarter-tone music, while of course the brass can also do so using the half-positions of pistons in trumpets, horns and tubas and of the slide in trombones. Naturally it is equally inadvisable to write very fast quarter-tone passages for these instruments, especially for the brass, even if with trombones, for example, it is possible to play fractions of the quarter-tone series of harmonics, derived from a principal sound, by using the half-positions of the slide in a fast articulated glissando. But such quarter-tone passages can be performed at any desired tempo, whether fast or slow. In short we can agree that favourable conditions now exist to write instrumental music with quarter-tones, and these factors will be of great help to singers.

It is well known that singing in quarter-tones is quite common in the folk-songs of some countries, but the same cannot be said for Western music in general, confined for centuries to the false intonation of the tempered scale. But once singers can refer to a definite orchestral pitch in quarter-tones they quickly adapt themselves. There are beginning to be many singers accustomed to singing music which demands complete independence of intonation and it is certain that to them the presence of a correct orchestral pitch in quarter-tones will largely compensate for the increased difficulty in intonation of new intervals. As for instrumentalists, the performance of quarter-tone music does not present any excessive difficulty, and ceases to be unnatural once the players are well prepared. It is only a question of education and habit.

We should like to make one final observation on the use of quarter-tone sound amalgams, created by the nature of instruments themselves, and not by the composer's knowledge or imagination (as in the case of normal chords). This is an event which occurs, we believe, for the first time in the history of instrumental music, and it can therefore be assumed that this affects the very creation of music. Particularly because in the field of quarter-tone music in which we are working, there are not yet any theories which can be the basis for a harmonic discipline. It is therefore of prime importance that the composer can make use of harmonic material in quarter-tones, the exact formation of which is beyond dispute, because it is natural. This allows the use of sound amalgams in ways which good taste and instinct may dictate, without the need to concern oneself with their individual harmonic components. The formulation of theories can wait. For the moment we need to stress that the possibilities of quarter-tones which we have considered can lead to a renewed interest in the organic correlations between the three parameters of music —harmony, melody and timbre—a correlation, particularly between harmony and melody, which was inevitably regarded as broken since the arrival of atonalism.

Those who believe, as I do, that the future of instrumental music is tied up with a greater exploitation of the harmonic components of sound, will see the technical developments of woodwind as a fundamental point of reference for a general advance in this direction by all the instruments of the orchestra. This appears to be the really basic problem which is of such great interest to the contemporary composer.

If we consider the sound material that was used to compose the music of the past, we must agree that man has needed few, but nevertheless essential, elements to create masterpieces—a maximum quantity of twelve sounds and, as far as quality is concerned, made up only of fundamental sounds and the overtones derived from them in well-known ways. If we compare this sound material with that produced by either a synthesizer or computer, we have a clear idea of the gulf between the past and the future, that is, of the great freedom of effect that orchestral instruments can offer. That is not to say that instruments are now intended to produce whatever is within the possibilities of electronic devices, but rather to preserve their *raison d'être* in the creative world of music by continuing to provide the composer with new and original sound material. In this sense it seems to us—and not only to us—that orchestral instruments still have ample freedom of action between the realities of the present and the possibilities of the future.

We hope therefore that the results of our researches will continue to be as favourably received in the musical world as on their first appearance, and that they will represent a small contribution towards the future of instrumental music.

# editor's note on acoustics

It may well be asked how a single instrumental tube can produce a number of complex sounds simultaneously. Conventional acoustics seems to have no ready explanation. Yet we have only to observe normal instrumental behaviour closely in order to conjecture how chords, broken sounds, etc., are produced.

A single sound produced by a wind instrument is already a complex of a large number of tones. A low note played loudly will consist of a fundamental and probably more than two dozen partials of sufficient strength to be measurable on the sound spectrograph. Some partials are as loud as the fundamental, yet we are accustomed to hearing the result as one sound of definite pitch only.

Woodwind have therefore always produced multiple sounds, but these have never had the strongly chordal character of those here described. To explain the generation of genuine chords, reference must be made to three factors—air-column behaviour, reed behaviour, and the influence of the 'formant'.

Players will already know the function of speaker keys. These are placed in the tube at such points that, when opened, they encourage the air column to vibrate in such a way as to produce the first harmonic (with the clarinet, the second harmonic). Players will know also that opening the first or second left-hand finger hole as well as the speaker key will cause the air column to vibrate in shorter segments so as to produce higher harmonics, to obtain higher notes. It is therefore evident that opening side (chromatic) keys or finger holes while others are closed (as, for example, in 'multiphonic' fingerings) has the effect of encouraging the air-column vibrations to divide into small parts (aliquot segments of the longest sound-wave) and therefore *enhance* certain partial tones, while others remain subdued. In fact, the open holes coincide with the position of the *nodes* in the various vibration-waves in the air column. If, for example, the open holes correspond with node positions of the seventh, tenth, fifteenth, and nineteenth partials, these sounds will be produced separately with facility. In fact, we have already seen (Chapter 2) how one fingering can produce several different harmonic sounds.

It is evident that if certain partials are enhanced in this way, while others are subdued because the open holes do not correspond with their nodes, the fundamental tone will appear to have an unfamiliar tone colour, particularly if the subdued partials are those which contribute strongly to the normal tone spectrum. This explains the different tone colours obtainable with the new technique.

The formation of chords is probably due to such fingerings, which permit the sounding of certain partials and the elimination of others. This explains the discordant character of most chords produced, as the higher partials are notes which, in many cases, have little direct harmonic relationship between themselves or with the fundamental. In fact, in most chords the true fundamental is not necessarily present and the enhanced partials, being of more or less equal volume, can be sounded together.

But this explanation of the sounding of chords seems incomplete. Even though a given fingering may enhance a number of partials, it is not certain why we can sound them together at a volume which would seem to be considerably more than that usual in upper partials. From practical observation it seems that reed behaviour is also a determining factor.

In conventional acoustics the reed is regarded as a generator, setting the air-column 'resonator' in motion in a way which is uniform and unchanging. Any possible change in reed behaviour is disregarded. But every player knows that the reed must be made to vibrate in sympathy with sounds, so that adjustments in embouchure, lip and air pressure are constantly necessary, particularly when changing register. These adjustments cause the reed to vibrate in different ways and players are well aware of the 'feel' of different vibrations. In passing from a single sound to a chord the player will feel a distinct change in reed behaviour. This is even more noticeable in playing broken sounds, the reed assuming a very exaggerated mode of vibration. It is therefore evident that though the precise contribution of the reed in emitting chords, broken sounds, etc., cannot be determined, reed behaviour plays a very prominent part.

The influence of the 'formants' in producing the new sounds is uncertain. It has been found that in wind instruments certain high notes tend to be reinforced by formants or selective resonances in the instrumental tube, that is, the tube responds to certain frequencies and reinforces them with its own mechanical resonance. It is probable that these frequencies play some part in multiphonic effects and in producing certain tone colours, as they will tend to make themselves evident whenever conditions permit.

Though it is impossible to indicate the exact derivation of multiphonic and other effects, it is obvious from these short notes that the player, in order to explore the fingerings needed for multiple sounds, must investigate those fingerings which encourage the sounding of upper partials (that is, fingerings which alternate closed and open sections of tube in order to facilitate the formation of the nodes of partial vibrations), coupled with an embouchure, lip and air pressure which will encourage the emission of such sounds. Close observation of reed behaviour will be essential in order to gain complete control of such an uncertain yet dominant factor in the production of the new sounds.

# 'Collage'

*Examples of music for each instrument as recorded on the accompanying disc*

*Note:* In this example and in Ex. 27, an unorthodox musical notation has been used, particularly as regards the duration and volume of sounds.

The duration of sounds is indicated by the length of the horizontal line attached to the stem of each note, so that the 'rhythm' of a phrase is derived from the proportions of the spaces between one note and another. Obviously, no metre is present.

Where the horizontal line joins several note stems, this does not necessarily mean that the notes should be played legato. Slurs are used to indicate legato, and where slurs are omitted, but the horizontal line is unbroken, the player should use soft tonguing so as to separate the notes slightly. Where the horizontal line is broken between notes, this indicates a silence in proportion to the length of the linear break.

Sometimes an over-all tempo indication is given (such as the *Andamento Lento* of Ex. 27), but in some cases this is omitted, so that the performer is left to interpret the music as he wishes and to vary the general tempo as his fantasy dictates. The tempo is therefore flexible, so that no indications of 'accelerando', 'rallentando', 'rubato', etc., are needed.

The volume of sounds is shown by the thickness of the horizontal line. A thin line is pianissimo, a very thick one fortissimo and so on. Crescendos, diminuendos, and fluctuations of volume are shown by corresponding variations in the thickness of this line.

In general, conventionally shaped round black notes indicate normal tone colours. The white notes indicating 'smorzato' effects have already been shown in Exx. 4 and 5, while the square black note has previously been used for 'broken' sounds in Ex. 22, etc. In Ex. 27 and 'Collage' there are other notes of different shapes which are associated with various tone colours and harmonic sounds. For example:

Oscillations of pitch are shown, and are usually associated with undulations of quarter-tones, though not always so. Variations in the velocity or 'intensity' of trills are shown by a graphic method which is self-explanatory.

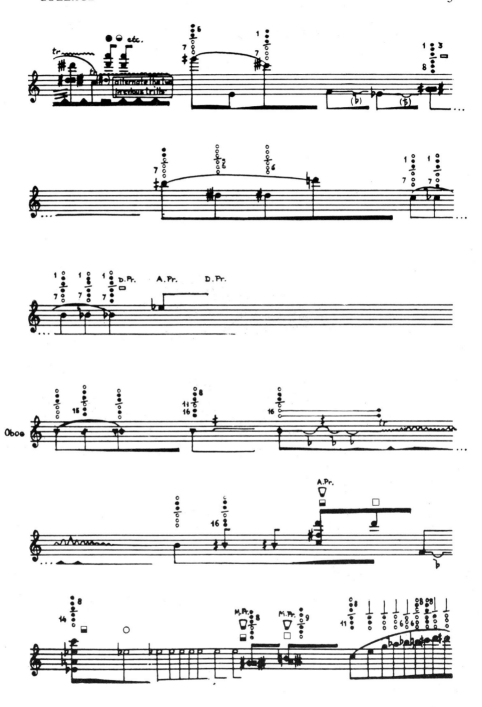

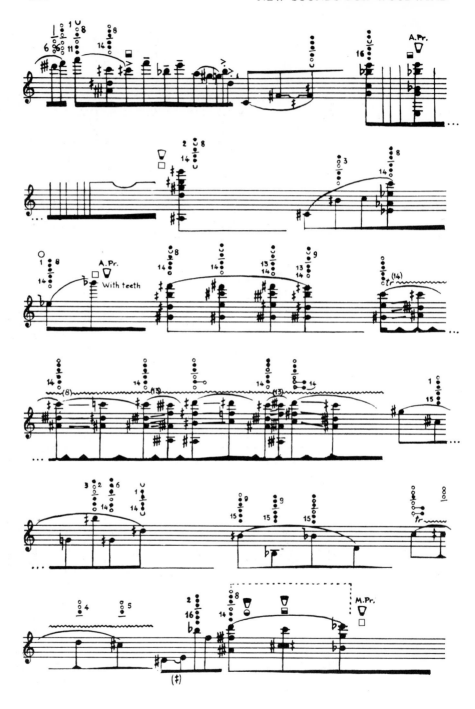

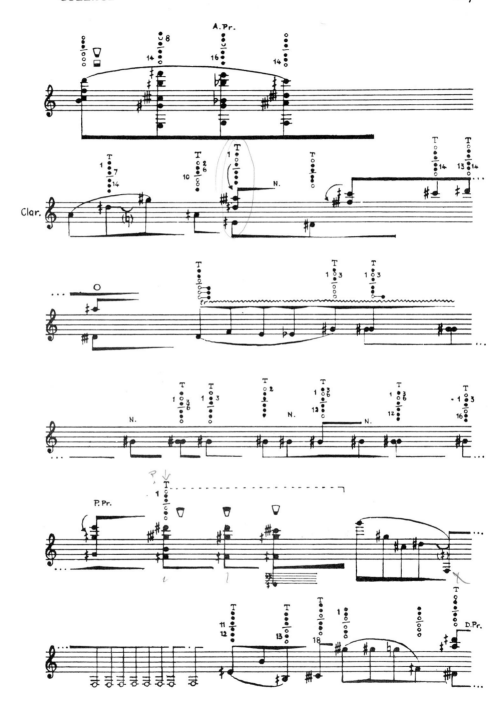

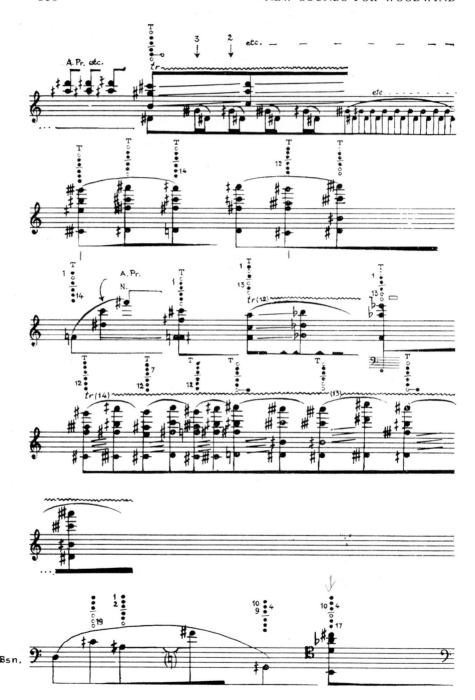

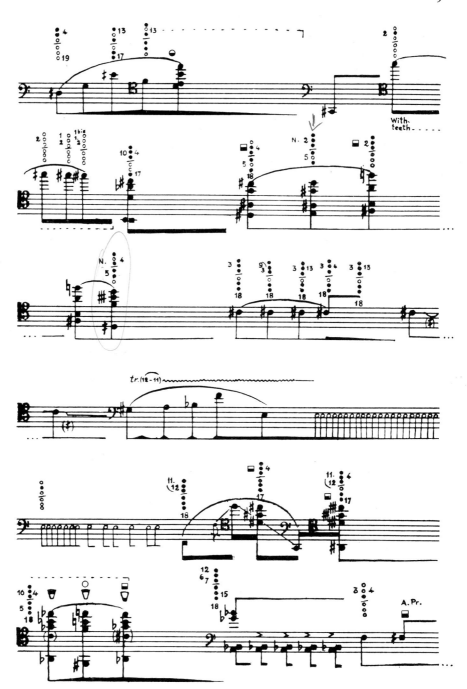

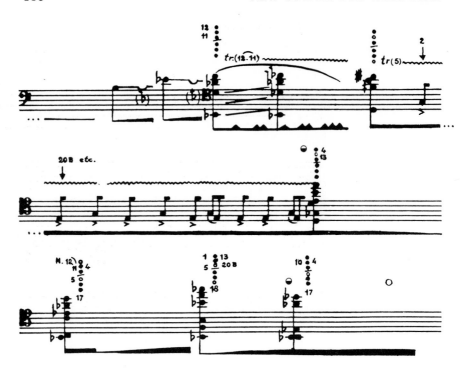

Andamento mosso

Flute

Oboe

Bb Clarinet

Bassoon

Andamento lento

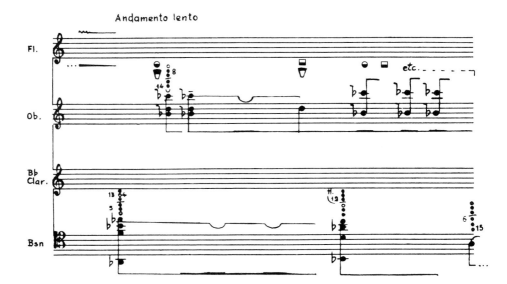

Fl.

Ob.

Bb Clar.

Bsn

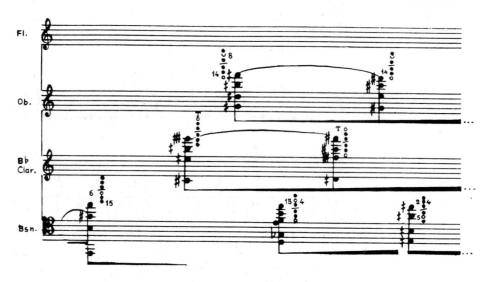

Andamento veloce

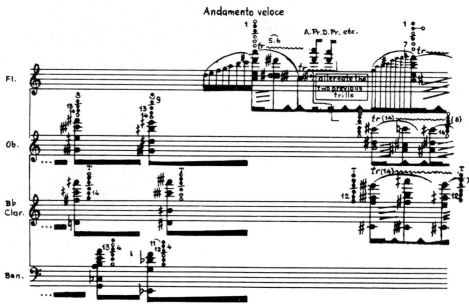